TRUMAN'S
GLEN

GREGORY WRIGHT

authorHOUSE®

AuthorHouse™
1663 Liberty Drive
Bloomington, IN 47403
www.authorhouse.com
Phone: 1 (800) 839-8640

Published by AuthorHouse 09/10/2019

ISBN: 978-1-7283-2175-2 (sc)
ISBN: 978-1-7283-2174-5 (e)

Library of Congress Control Number: 2019910936

Print information available on the last page.

ABOUT THE AUTHOR

With the publishing of his second novel, he writes about the complications of a young man's behavior and the fallout out from those acts. Having written over a dozen short stories for anthologies in the genre of literary fiction, he enjoys creating stories involving people that are dealing with the consequences of impetuous decisions and how they deal with the drama that that follows. Using unique characters with complexities of their own to enrich the stories, he adds to it a thin veil of mystery using a style of writing that creates an entertaining and enriched story that reveals everyone's connection.

CHAPTER I

As Michael lay in his work clothes (grey dockers, pressed white collared shirt, unexceptional low-styled brown shoes) in the warm afternoon sun, he adjusted himself while the aluminum lawn chair beneath him creaked and scraped against the concrete from his every movement. Being in his early twenties, a day like this was what he yearned for. Slipping out of work without his supervisors knowing and squirreling away on his back patio. He had just started the job, his first full time one in a while and felt that after a few months of 'new' guy pressure, he deserved this.

It was unusually warm October day, even more of a reason to sneak out of work early (like 4 hours early) on a Tues. Not only to enjoy the sunshine but also spend a little time with his five year old son who was playing in the backyard and to make every attempt not to be where he was supposed to be. There was too much to consider, too much to plan, and yet few places to hide. His youth was expressed by a keen eye coupled with a sharp instinct for opportunity. It also manifested itself with rashness and a poor sense of choice.

He felt the vibration on his belt from his phone as a call came in. He had it ID'd as the Repairs shop, but it was really an acquaintance he preferred to keep anonymous. Someone who usually starts work late and finishes very late, but in this instance needed to speak to him now. Someone who also viewed the football game last night, much as a broker views a commodities screens very intensely. "Yes?" he said as he opened the screen.

As he sat there with the phone, listening, he watched his two-year-old daughter wander out onto the patio and struggle to climb up a small plastic slide, foregoing the usual ascent of stairs, and trying to mimic her five-year-old brother who was already at the top and impatiently waiting for her to move.

While this drama was unfolding under his neglectful eye, he continued holding his cell phone closer to his ear. Closer actually than what was necessary because he didn't want anyone to hear the voice on the other end; the voice that spoke deliberately and clearly so there was no mistaking it's intent.

"You see,…." It continued with a faintly detectable Eastern European accent, "the risk taking events we had an agreement on yesterday didn't work in your favor, and I have decided that we are not going to deal with this like before." His hand began to sweat and his stomach churned as he recalled the winning field goal going through the uprights and the demise of the point spread he had hoped to make fluttered down in pieces around him like so much confetti. "When you add that up with the other losses from the weeks before, you now owe a substantial amount of money, of which a certain percentage of say $15,000 id due by tomorrow afternoon......... at 5:00."

"I need more time for that kind of money." He didn't recognize his own voice it was so harsh and raspy. Desperate. He hadn't expected the note to be called in. He definitely hadn't expected it to be paid so quickly.

"There is no more time. In fact if we do not receive full restitution soon, I will be forced to send ..." he seemed to search for the word "......collectors." The voice suddenly changed, became more subtle, more convincing, almost understanding. "Please Michael, don't force me to do this, it is something that once it's in motion, I cannot stop."

By now, his daughter had ascended halfway up the slide; by learning not to stand upright and that by leaning into the slide she had the advantage. But his son was intent on going down and his expression changed from impatience to an intensely hard star, like the cheetah before the gazelle, the eagle over the rabbit, as the otter above the clam.

"I understand." Michael replied slowly

"Now I can expect a payment tomorrow?"

A pause. "Yes."

"Excellent, I will meet your tomorrow at the usual place. Don't be late, I have somewhere else to be." The phone clicked.

As if on cue, his son launched himself down the slide, not a push, or an easy slip away, but a butt in the air, arms fully extended head- leaning-forward-for-torque launch. In the short distance to where his sister was, he smiled the satisfying smile of the fresh kill. The 'free shot.'

With two bodies now in motion, physics intervened. Upon striking his sister she didn't fall backwards or over the side as intended, but instead pitched forward, feet rising behind her, chest landing on his son's chest, and the solid bullet of her forehead striking the soft pliable cartilage of the boy's nose.

The loud pop that ensured was followed by that sudden quiet, the stillness of an accident spent of energy and of the victims assessing the damage. Pushing his sister off him, the boy pushed on his nose and brought away a palm full of rich, dark blood. Eyes widening, he began to scream, and then rose to run into the house, away from the crime scene and his fatherly witness and to his compassionate and understanding mother.

The daughter, now screaming and crying for no other reason than she saw her brother doing it, also ran into the house, leaving Michael with an empty yard, and newly ringing cell phone and a bloody handprint on a pink plastic slide.

Slightly numb from the collector's phone call and the shock of the assault, he mechanically touched the 'receive' button of the cell phone without checking the caller ID.

"Hello." He began.

Silence. "Where are you?' a calm, female voice asked from the airwaves.

"Uh….' He began, then suddenly pulled the phone away to ID the number. Recognizing it as his office, the tone and pitch of the voice suddenly matched his own mental ID – that of the office manager.

Suddenly, as if in a play, the children returned to the

stage, screaming as loud, if not louder into a phone receiver he was now holding in the air. Turning around to try and quiet them, he instead turned into a very frustrated wife in a sleeveless grey T-shirt with the words "Muldoons St. Pats 07" in green lettering across the front and size 6 capris pants desperately trying to corral size 8 thighs.

"Damn it Mike, if you're going to be home, at least watch the kids so they don't kill each other!" she then applied the cold water compress in her hand to a sniffling boy with a hemorrhaged nose, while she calmly patted her daughter's head with her other hand to soothe her.

Michael looked away from the triage scene and at the thin, black phone, literally a scalpel in his hand which he was now required to hold next to his neck. The phone was only as wide as two fingers and the weight of a pencil, yet it suddenly felt foreign and heavy, like a brick or a loaded gun. Bringing it back to his ear, he heard only sharp steady breathing on the other side of the line.

"Hummmm….." he began again.

"Michael, please be in my office at 8:00 am on Monday", and then those terminally parting words. "…with all your files." A sharp click ended any reply.

Folding it slowly, he laid it on his lap, and gazed again at the slide with the bloody handprint now having already dried hard from the late afternoon sun.

"Look, Mike," she began again, moving the crimson rag from one hand to the other as she delicately dabbed at the child's nose. "I ordered a pizza for dinner, and you need to pick it up."

"Ok." He replied sheepishly, having slide so far in his

chair, he was almost laying down. Numb, he watched his daughter skip away from her mother, the trauma long forgotten as her brother stared at her, the cold hard stare of a man wrongly punished. Looking up, he noticed the same stare from his wife. She was holding the bloody rag out along with her other bloody hand, fingers extended.

It was a cold, dark unforgiving look and it expected recognition, now, like a rabbi that just performed his own circumcision.

"How about going now!" she darted, nodding sharply at each syllable to express the point.

"I'm still cleaning up your mess."

Sullenly he stood up and shuffled through the house slowly, waiting for the three parting statements as he strode through the kitchen and towards the garage.

"Pick up the dry cleaning while you are at it." One.

"And don't forget napkins!' Two.

Reaching the door to the garage, he placed his and on the knob and hesitated.

"And when you're there, call me and read me the menu. I may want something different!!"

"Ok." He threw back to her, to be reassuring, then slapped the garage door opener by the side of the door and fished his keys out of his front pocket.

The 10-year-old yellow Chevy sat squarely in the middle of the garage, large and bulbous like a toad. It was his wife's car, she got it when she was 16 and as long as it kept running there was no need to trade it in; at least that was her thinking. He had tried to get her to trade it in a number of times, but to no avail. When it came down to it, she had too much attachment to it.

Too many memories for her to give away.

Angling around the stacks of boxes and toys stored around the walls of the garage, (hence the car in the middle of the garage), he was able to angle around the side, open the door a bit and slide into the driver's seat. As if stepping into a time capsule, the cold smell of the plastic leather seats filled his lungs as he squirmed to get comfortable in the well-worn driver's seat. The sunlight slowly crept over the trunk and into the backseat as the garage door reached its apex, then held. Turning over the engine, he waited until the serpentine belt quit slipping and then engaged reverse, allowing the car to slowly slide out of the garage and into the driveway.

The neighborhood was a copy of any other neighborhood, and truly a copy in many ways. The only difference in design begin either two or three bedroom, and where the utility closet was located. All had small roofed mailboxes shaped like barns, and simple, understated front stoop, barely able to keep one person out of the rain, and a pitched roof with an octagonal window in the center, which, being in the attic where no one goes was of no use to anyone. And everything was white. A ghostly, never-ending factory white, stretching for miles of curved streets and cul-de-sacs with names straight out of Mother Goose and Aesop.

Pulling into the street, he turned the wheel, put it in drive and drove slowly across the front of his house. Not to get a view of the stateliness of his home, he was going to pass about 200 units just like his to get that fix. No, just to view the new Buick he had parked on the curb. A car he received six months ago when he landed the job, and which he will almost certainly be giving up on Monday. It reminded him to clean out the trunk over the weekend. Get the chairs, blankets, and child seats out of there before then.

Gunning the engine, he started to race up the street, only to catch the watchful glare of parents walking along the sidewalk, standing in their front yard, or washing a car in the driveway. The watchful stare of the 'Overlords of Justice" he liked to call them with their unseen hand of jurisprudence, willing him to maintain the 15 mph speed limit as he progressed towards the main entrance of the Sweetwater subdivision. Unable to overcome their subtle objections, he let the engine idle down from 25 to the required speed and smiled at them as he rolled pass praying the engine wouldn't die of boredom and watching a runaway dog speed past in its own bid for freedom. He truly hoped the dog would make it. Secretly, he wanted to be that dog.

As he rounded the first curve, his phone rang. Instinctively knowing who it was this time, he reached to his hip, snapped it off and flipped it open in one motion.

"Yes." he began.

"Please check on my dad, I didn't have time today. I know you hate his stories, but try to see if he needs anything."

"Shall I read him the menu to see if there is anything he wants?"

"Not funny asshole, just do it."

He clicked the phone off and tossed it on the passenger seat as he reached the first stop sign. Turning left, he amused himself by repeating her last words practicing new annunciations and dialects.

"Not…..funny…..asshole." he finished with a cowboy accent as he reached the driveway to the townhouse where his father –in-law lived. "Not….funny….asshole." he said as a Native American, finishing with, "Not…..funny…asshole." in a rich Pakistani dialect; definitely his best voice.

He knocked once on the door, waited silently, squinting at the blinding white concrete sidewalk, the white vinyl siding and the short, clay gnome which was holding his finger to his pink lips in a hush while holding a small sign warning 'An old Gramp lives here.'

Not getting a response, he knocked again while turning the knob and pushing in. "Hello!" he yelled as he walked into a small living room. There was some furniture there, a lime green sofa with threadbare arms, a small entertainment center with an antiquated television in the center. A worn leather recliner was at an angle from it, with a small quilt folded over the back, and two remotes placed on the seat. Standing next to it was a lamp with a small table, built into the center with a stand at about armrest height. It all seemed to be forced into the room and as he walked past the lamp and into the kitchen he struck it with his hand, knocking over some worn books about the American Civil War and a thin book of German poems, in German.

Picking them up he slide the books back in place, and walked into a spotless kitchen, with the exception of a small collection of forks clustered at the bottom of the sink. The counters were clear, the small dining room table set nicely with pepper and salt shaker in the middle of the kitchen seemed clean and orderly. Nothing out of place.

He noted in his inspection report to his wife that her dad of 83 years was eating, reading on a constant basis, and cleaning up after himself. Now as long as he didn't find him face down in the bathroom, everything would check out.

He didn't get as far as the bedroom. Noticing that the patio door was open slightly, he walked towards it and saw the old man with is back to him; seated on the grass in a wicker chair. A tan freckled scalp betrayed years of working outside, and as he traversed the small concrete patio to head towards the man, he saw a small stream of water suddenly arch up above the old man's head and out onto the lawn.

Suddenly feeling like an intruder, Michael barked out the old man's name. "Joseph!" at which point, the grandfather turned in his seat, his face twisted with thick glasses askew as if in a funhouse mirror. A garden hose was firmly in his hand on his lap, he tilted the stream of water downward upon turning to look at his visitor.

"Ya Michael!' he bellowed in a voice as strong as his spirit.

Relieved that this wasn't a urination moment, Michael strode next to him sliding his hands into his pockets and watched as Joseph turned his attention back to the object he was watering; a small whip of a tree, barely six feet with thick oversized leaves and a questionable will to live.

"Nice tree." Michael said.

"Ya…" Joseph answered with a slow nod. "It is a maple." The words barely distinct through the heavy German accent.

"I'm surprised they let you plant it." Michael looked up and gazed at the huge expanse of open grass between Joseph's house and the line of homes on his side, facing the line of homes across from him, their patio doors all facing each other. Michael likened them to the lines of a football team with offense and defense squared off opposite each other and a forty-yard neutral zone in between. With no allowances for fences, the ends stretched for hundreds of yards, the exact location of property lines known only to county surveyors, guidance satellites, and the dogs shocked by the invisible fence.

"I didn't ask anyone, I just buy it and plant it. Let them come and get me."

There was a small silence as Michael stood there, not sure how to mention to Joseph about the 'Overlords' and their invisible hands of liens, petitions, and their mastery of the knowing look. As if anticipating a remark, Joseph looked up. The thick glasses he wore failed to dim the sharp Arctic blue of his eyes and the thin wrinkles on his face seemed wooden as his lips drew narrow and his grip tightened on the hose. "My house, my land,…..my America." He then returned to his watering as the leaves caught a slight breeze and the tree bent over helplessly, struggling to regain its posture once the breeze had subsided.

"Well………." Michael began, but then was unsure where to go. "good luck with that."

Michael added quickly to end the awkward pause. "Andrea asked me to see if you wanted anything. I'm going to pick up some dinner at Angelo's and I could drop it by, or you could come over."

Joseph looked at him slyly, "No thank you." He said softly. "I need to finish a book tonight."

"Well, it's just a book, it can wait right? The words aren't going anywhere."

Joseph now began to wiggle the hose, causing he stream of water to break apart and slap against the grass. "I wish to finish it because I believe there is a truth in the ending."

"What's the name of the book, maybe I've read it?"

"I doubt it." Joseph said. "As I said it is a book with a truth." Having watched the water puddle appreciably at his feet, Joseph switched the small shut off valve at the end of the hose to off. Rising from the chair, his legs spread shoulder width to gain balance he reached his full stature although still at an angle and began to coil the hose in a bear paw of a hand as he walked back to the house.

"When was the last time you read a book?" Joseph asked, his meaty hands firmly holding the hose.

Michael thought solemnly. "Before the kids." When actually it was possibly years before that. Possible high school.

"Andrea worries too much about me." He said forcefully changing the subject as he followed the hose back to the spigot on the back of the house. "Tell her I'll call her when I am finished."

"Tonight?" Michael asked.

Joseph slipped the hose on a green bracket screwed to the side of the house, the metal shrinking from the weight of the water still in the hose.

"Perhaps…." He answered, then entered the back of the house and disappeared into the kitchen. Obediently Michael followed, closing the patio door behind him and returning his hands to his pockets. Reviewing the kitchen again, where Joseph was headed, he jangled his keys in his pocket, in an action of anticipation, of what he wasn't sure.

As Joseph leaned over the kitchen sink, he turned the water on to wash his hands. "Stop doing that." He barked without looking up, the water flowing over the knuckles, soap bubbling quickly with a vigorous twisting of his hands. He then turned to face Michael, reaching for the dish rag hanging on a rack on the cabinet door beneath the sink. "It is annoying." he said, finishing the thought.

Standing before him, Michael was always amazed at the full measure of the man. Old men always seemed to be made of parts, none of them adding up to a whole. Joseph had worked for years in the factories on the south side at a time when if you needed a job, you just knocked on the door. If that didn't work out, or he got laid off, you just walked next door. Andreas used to tell him about days remembering days when he would leave for work in one uniform, and come home in another.

Machinery of any type or shape was his vocation.

Drill presses were what he loved and spent the most time on. His hands seemed to be an odd shade of grey from the oils and shavings, the knuckles knotted from use, yet with enough tensile strength that Michael would watch him crack peanuts between them. The palms were thick, very thick like a baseball mitt, and the hands trailed back to hambone forearms and biceps deceptively small, but sinewy strong.

They were still a young man's arms, yet they preceded a thin crest of a chest, and a perfectly round bulbous stomach beneath. The legs were reed like and stiff, as if they had become the steel carriage of the drills he had worked on for years. A stooped back hide narrow shoulders, but it wasn't a debilitative spine, just years of carrying and bending. It even seemed to propel him forward at a faster pace wherever he went. It was the engine to his drive.

"Come with me." He barked. Not waiting for a reply, he turned and walked out of the kitchen and through the living room into a small hallway leading to the back of the house. Michael obediently followed, his hands still deep in his pockets, but careful not to jingle his keys.

In the rear of the house were two bedrooms, one for Joseph, and other similar but much smaller. Joseph pushed through the closed door with Michael close behind. The curtains were closed, and rather than open them to let in the sunlight, Joseph clicked on the light. There before them were stacks and boxes of books. Some in narrow columns like apiaries. Michael could only stand in the doorway amazed as the old man negotiated the narrow path between them in search of something in particular.

"So that's what was in those boxes." Michael exclaimed. "I saw the movers cramping up as the hauled them in."

Joseph didn't seem to hear him as he moved one particular box and shuffled through the one beneath it. Slipping through a few volumes, he produced three paperbacks, held firmly in his grip like he was pulling a puppy from a bucket.

Turning to face Michael, he turned his hand up, so the binding of the books was evident. They were old and worn, brown with age, but the letters of the titles shown clearly in gold and red.

"Pick one." Joseph said.

Michael cautiously leaned over and glanced at the titles.

"<u>Catcher in the Rye</u>" Joseph said.

"Sorry, don't know much about baseball." Was Michael's answer.

Joseph winced as if stuck by a needle in the ear.

"<u>Fahrenheit 451.</u>" continued Joseph. "Do you like stories about firemen??"

"Not really."

"That was a trick question." Joseph returned. Michael just shrugged.

"How about <u>Lord of the Flies?</u>" Joseph hoped.

"You know, I was pretty good in history, I'll take that one. I like knights and stuff."

Joseph eagerly separated it from the other two and handed it to Michael. As Michael opened it a flipped through the pages, his eye caught sight of a thin volume on the top of a nearby stack.

"How about this one?" he asked, picking up the book to see the title more clearly. "Finnegan's Wake."

Joseph eagerly reached out and snatched the book away from his grasp. "No, not that one Michael. You'll just hurt yourself."

Michael shrugged again as he left the room, paging through his assigned book while being hustled out by Joseph.

"Now you tell that daughter of mine that I am just fine. If one day I'm not here, it just means I moved back to the old neighborhood."

Michael looked over his shoulder at a seemingly pursuant Joseph as he replied.

"Don't say that Pops, you'll just piss her off and you know who'll she'll take it out on…………"

By now they had reached the door, and Joseph stopped and stood, his arms reaching out to the doorframe, standing like a paratrooper before a jump.

"Careful young man." He warned. "when you read that book you'll understand more of the world in which we live in whether you want to or not."

Michael gave him a faraway shrug as he slid behind the wheel, tossing the book onto the passenger seat as he turned the key and engaged the car. Pulling out of the driveway, he slowed in front of the town house, waved once again, then headed out of the complex and towards the pizza parlor.

Joseph watched him disappear; then felt suddenly

serene. It was an odd feeling to him, and he wasn't sure how to cope with it. In the past, he would head over to the tavern for a few hours, or the diner that was on the corner that had been by his house in the old neighborhood, possibly even to Rudolph's house to sit on the patio to watch the sunset. But now, he just took a deep breath, glanced around the neighborhood, and closed the door.

On the drive to the restaurant, Michael began to take stock in all the trouble he was in. The wife's anger was manageable, the disappointment from his kids, usual. But the money trouble with the 'outfit' that was bad, really bad. The soon lack of a job will add more wood to the flames, and could make the wife issues desperate.

Still, recovering from the shock of the last few hours, his mind was beginning to calm down and he was looking for ways to get out. The job thing he could negotiate. Get a new one before he told his wife about losing the old one. But the money he needed to get out of trouble without losing a few digits, or possible a limb seemed insurmountable.

He couldn't get the money from relatives without raising suspicions. He couldn't stand it, and he had nothing to sell or funds to draw from without anyone knowing. What he needed was time. " Let's start with that.", he said out loud, as he approached the restaurant.

The restaurant wasn't that far from Josef's house and within ten minutes he was pulling into the second tier parking spaces marked out in the center of the parking lot with thick yellow paint. The restaurant was good size, it easily fit two hundred people and it looked close to its capacity as he walked towards the front door. Located in the outlot of a relatively new mall it already had changed over four times. First a deli/cafe which the health dept. shut down after six months, then a gaming store, which the internet put out of business, then as a Chinese restaurant which INS put out of business after someone informed about the work force and the lack of paperwork there of. This final evolution, into an Italian restaurant, seems to be the one that is working as the place was full of patrons, the food on the counters was moving quickly and the register was constantly ringing.

Sliding behind a large group of people waiting to pay and pleasantly arguing about their favorite ingredients, he glanced ahead and calculated how many longer it would take. Noticing he attendant struggling with the credit card slider, he looked around and noticed the ATM by one of the pillars near the restrooms. Deciding cash would get him out of here faster, he navigated around the tables, running children and chasing parents. As he was about to reach the machine, he was suddenly shoved into a small table where a young man sat with her two small children. Alarmed she instinctively reached across the table to protect them while giving him a stern facial warning.

"Sorry." He mumbled as he quickly turned to face his attacker.

"Hey cos!" came the challenge as Michael faced his first cousin on his mother's side. They weren't close, their relationship was based mostly in half nelson's and wedgies, rather than meaningful advice on relationships. Still, they seemed to be near each other in their lives, Riley only lived two subdivisions over and although neither actively sought the other, their paths seemed to cross frequently.

"Christ, Riley!" He exclaimed regaining his balance. "You almost made me take out that table!"

"I would have grabbed you before that happened. Riley exclaimed as he gazed at the table and winked at the mom. She turned away shaking her head in disgust while mopping up one of the spilled lemonades on the table. "What are you doing here? Where's the tribe."

"Andrea ordered a pizza for me to get. Why are you here? You don't have any kids." "Just here with some of the softball team having a few beers. Hey! Come and join us for a few, they will keep the pizza hot for you."

"Nay, I need to get back." But Riley was already looking away, noticeably at a young waitress by the cash register.

"Looking for your next ex-wife?" Michael chimed in.

Riley smiled wirily. "Nay, just chasing tail." He then glanced at Michael disapprovingly as he noticed they were wearing similar shorts, sport socks and white tennis shoes. "Dude, he suddenly added, we look too much alike, your distorting the atmosphere. I'll be in touch." And with that, he began to work his way through the crowd towards the brunette sorting her order tickets by the register.

Resuming his trek to the cash machine, he reached for his wallet as he stood n front of the screen. Punching in his ode, he gazed around the dining room. When t came to the authorization screen, he was preparing to punch in his amount button when heard the screaming.

"Gas!! Gas!!" was heard from somewhere and then suddenly a short bald man in a cook's apron came bolting out of the basement door, just behind the counter. He had a wild look of fear in his eyes and he took two more steps when Michael could see the specter of fire lurching behind him.

Everything now seemed to move in slow motion, The flame was only the pilot, as the entire kitchen behind the counter suddenly seemed to lurch forward, pushing the counter forward into the crowd. He heard only a millisecond of the explosion as the enormity of the blast shattered his ear drum and the rush of heat singed the left side of his face.

Instinctively he ducked behind the pillar as all around him he could see tables and chairs thrown past him and through the large glass windows behind him. Shards of broken glass and plates swooshed past him like scythes as they cut into and through people. Dust suddenly enveloped him and he closed his eyes and covered his mouth as pulverized drywall surrounded him, then he felt a push on his shoulder as the hanging ceiling above him collapsed on top of him. Instinctively he covered his eyes and lowered his head, letting the weight of the ceiling push him down.

When he felt the wind had passed, he slowly removed his hands and cracked his eyes open. A haze filled the room, and as it began to slowly slip out of the broken front windows, he could see the devastation more clearly. Nothing around him seemed familiar. The walls around him that had been painted a fiesta red and white were now scorched black. All of the debris had been pushed from the back of the restaurant to the front where the all that remained were the thick panes of the front glass had collected around it.

As he looked behind him, he could see out the front windows where more tables and chairs had landed, and in the middle of the parking lot the blackened corpse of the short man who had raised the alarm. Around the floor he could now see a carpet of bodies, some twitching, others rolling in pain and others lying perfectly still. His right ear could still hear somewhat, and the moaning and crying began to crescendo, balancing out the humming in his left.

As the fog cleared, he could now see people rushing in from the front, trying to uncover and reach the wounded people buried in the rubble. Yelling for more help from the rescuers now began to increase as the amount of wounded began to become aware they were injured. Being the only man standing in the dining room, he was easily ignored as those that were unaffected scrambled around trying to help out those that were on the ground.

Feeling a slight stinging in his legs, he looked down and saw blood seeping out of small cuts and gouges. It flowed in the thick red streams from the deepest cuts, while thin rivulets ran down through the hair on his legs, combining in patches of red at his ankles. A deep cut in his thigh poured profusely and he could feel the sticky wetness of blood collecting in his shoe.

But in a sudden moment of awareness, he realized he was still standing. No broken bones, no deep gouges or arterial ruptures. Pushing his hands through his hair, he felt the chalky dryness of cooked limestone, the powdery remnants of the cardboard ceiling, and oddly enough as he entangled it from his hair, the bowl end of a black plastic spoon. Staring at it vacantly, he was pushed aside by two young men helping a middle aged woman through the debris. As they led her out slowly by her arms, he could see jagged cuts going down her face and blood trailing out of her ears. The shock had numbed her, silently she followed whomever was leading her. Michael watched as a thick bubble of mucus and blood formed at the end of her nose, popping in a thick film over her mouth just as she passed by.

The debris in the air had started to collect in his eyes and he rubbed them to get some clarity. Pulling his upper lid over his lower eyelash, while looking down, he was able to begin to focus. The ground came in more clearly and as he blinked an image appeared before him. A leg lay partially covered by a table top, it's shoe clearly visible while where it ended was very abrupt and unattached. The pants leg was similar to his, and he inhaled quickly at the thought that it was his own. But the two he needed were firmly beneath him, and tis third, although amazingly similar in size and dress was an orphan, an obedient limb having been violently separated from its position. As the skin congealed and cooled; turning gray from the lack of attachment, Michael saw something else. A gentle glow, a mild dim slowly increasing the longer he stared at it, and like Excalibur itself, he saw an answer before him to all the troubles in the kingdom.

Looking around again, he noticed he still had the same animity as before, and with that power of invisibility, he reached into his back pocket for his wallet, removed it with his finger and thumb, holding it in front of him, he hesitated. Around him sirens were blaring and doors were slamming. The yelling was becoming more forceful and direct as volunteers and first responders now began in earnest to find survivors in the wreckage, all this despite the humming in his ears and the pain increasing from the cuts in his legs. Despite all the chaos around him, Michael deliberately released the wallet, watched as it turned end over end to the floor, landing with a bounce, and opening like a clam so that his picture ID, a license photo taken six years ago with the blank stare of accusation glaring back at him.

It landed perfectly by the shredded pants leg, near a pocket which it could have easily slipped out of. Michael stared at it for a second, then looked around one more time, sighed a path through the debris, and calmly walked, albeit unsteadily out of the restaurant and into the daylight. At the edge of the parking lot, he gazed one more time at the windshields blowout of the cars, the inside of the restaurant, now scattered all over the asphalt and the triage station where more than a dozen people had already gathered. Realizing he couldn't take his car, he walked past it, touched the hood as a last reminder of what he was leaving. Then turned the corner of the building and walked into the world of shadows.

Andrea heard the solid thud of the explosion as she was cleaning up the back patio. Sounding like a thick wall striking the ground, she gazed in the direction of the strip mall and watched as a thick black cloud blossomed out of the collection of houses, like a mushroom on the forest floor. Seconds later sirens began to filter through as the cloud began to fade into a tin feathery line of smoke, twisting and turning with the wind.

Having a sudden sick feeling, she darted into the house, skirted past her two children playing in the family room and avoided the pointed question from the oldest; "What was that boom mommy?" Reaching for the phone on the end table, she snatched it and quickly began dialing before disappearing behind the door leading into the laundry room. In her haste, she misdialed Michael's cell number, until finally, by using her thumbs rather than her quivering fingers she could hear it connect. Barely breathing, she could hear the rings, the gap between each one longer than the last, until it clicked. Ready to ask if he was okay, the voice mail appeared and left the tone for the massage.

At first, not knowing what to say, she just began. "Michael, please call me, I saw…something, a cloud of smoke and, and….I need to know if you are okay. Please, please call!!" She almost choked off the last few words then clicked the phone off. Pausing in the small white room, she tucked the phone under her cheek and closed her eyes tightly, willing it to ring with his call back, and willing herself not to cry.

When her composure was steady, she emerged to see two small, yet perceptive faces looking at her with large eyes and quizzical looks.

"Why are you so sad mommy?" her daughter asked.

"I'm not sad sweetheart, just a little concerned."

"Is it daddy?"

Andrea looked down at their two children, then looked away and out through the patio door. Seeing her neighbor Brenda and her little girl out on their patio, she took the initiative and followed her instinct.

"Look, Amy is out with her mom, I bet she would love it if you two came over to play with them."

Without the chance to reply, she had shoes on the children's feet and they were hustled out the patio door, and pulled across the grass easement to Brenda's house.

Brenda saw them coming, she also noticed the strain on Andre's face as she hustled her two charges across the lawn. She crossed her arms and smiled pleasantly as they approached the toy strewn concrete.

"I was wondering if we could come over and play for little while with Amy? Is that okay with Amy's mom?" Andrea asked in singsong as her eyes motioned to Brenda to the side. Amy, being an only child squealed with delight at the playmates and very quickly the trio was engaged as the moms pulled aside to talk.

"Can you watch them for a few hours?" Andrea asked.

"Sure, what's up?"

"There is something wrong with Michael." She tried to closed her eyes and fists as she tried to express herself. "I can just feel it."

"Did you try and reach him, where is he?"

Andrea opened her eyes and looked towards the thin

clouds in the distance, now turning white as the steam rose from the water from the fire hoses.

"He went to go get pizza," She hesitated. "and now he's not answering his phone." The tears began to return. "And I'm scared." And she took a deep breath to steady herself.

"I have the kids. I will keep them for as long as you like." Brenda assured her. "Just if you are going to go looking for hi, take someone with you." She hesitated. "You don't know what you'll find." Andrea nodded, kissed both kids on the head and darted across the greenway again.

Reaching the silence of the house, she immediately checked for messages, called Michael three more times, then grabbed her keys and purse and headed towards the garage. Pulling out on the apron of the driveway, she hesitated, put the car into park and dialed her father.

As if expecting the call, he picked up on the first ring. "Dad! I can't find Mike!"

"Come get me and we'll both go look." He said finishing her thought.

Feeling the strength of his fortitude, she quickly threw the car into gear and sped down the lane, swerving around groups of people previously occupied with speeding cars, now looking a the curiosity on the horizon.

Reaching her father's townhouse, she saw him impatiently waiting in the driveway. By the time she had pulled in and put the car into reverse, he was already in the passenger seat. With a shared look of concern, she sped out of the subdivision and towards the smoke.

As they drew closer to the strip mall, the chaos seemed to thicken as the curious, the first responders, and the ghouls with cell phone cameras gathered in hopes of catching a photo of a gruesome picture or an errant first responder; the price of which could be work thousands of dollars, were descending in a slow, cluttered mass.

"It is only going to get worse as we get closer," he said. Straining his neck to look around, he pointed to a pharmacy on the left. "Pull into the alley behind there, the lot is full, but no one will bother the car with everything else going on."

Obediently she weaved through the stalled traffic, hopping a curb at the last intersection, to reach the alley.

"Here!" her father yelled. "Here, here! No one will bother it here, and it looks like we are only a few blocks away."

Pulling to the side, they exited quickly and slipped into the mob of people struggling to witness the tragedy unfolding. Andrea was torn between running towards the fire and walking slowly so that her father would keep up. She ended up surging a number of yards, then retreating slightly to encourage her father. This ebb and flow continued, for the few blocks remaining to the restaurant. Finally, as they reached the edge of the parking lot, he motioned for her to go on with exaggerated wave of his massive hand. Now released from her charge, she ran ahead to the first policemen she saw and implored her passionate desire to be there as he nodded negatively and for a brief second grabbed her shoulders to steady her. Seeming to understand, the policeman then pointed over to a small tent on the perimeter where there was a collection of police and fire personnel discussing tactics and triage. Without thinking him, she darted over to the group and soon disappeared amongst the first responders.

When Joseph arrived, he was shocked by how close he was to the destruction. Now walking on broken glass and pieces of metal, he stopped before the policeman and gazed a the carnage before him.

From the fire, the center of the restaurant was black, sheets of black smoke had scarred the edges of the roof and firemen and evidence technicians were now beginning to walk through the debris, tagging and flagging anything of interest.

He too was stopped by the officer, but with a gift of distraction, a group of distraught parents pushed through the shallow yellow tape and rushed towards the scene. Choosing to help the other officers struggling to keep them back, the sentry left Joseph where he stood and trotted down towards the agitation on the boundary of the scene.

Taking the opportunity given to him, Josef slipped passed the tape and trotted behind a small paneled truck. Cautiously he approached the wreckage, darting behind vehicles and wreckage so as not to be seen. The chaos of the scene and the heavy influx of personnel made him less noticeable, however, he knew he had to look around quickly before someone noticed an eighty year old man walking amongst the debris.

He was so intent on being undetected, that when he reached the cars in the first parking spaces, he suddenly realized he was standing in front to of Michael's car. Hunched over in concealment, he now stood up straight in disbelief. The driver's side of the car faced the blast zone, and blackened paint was seared into the metal along with sharp barbs of metal from the chairs and building frame which had impaled into the side. The windows on that side had blown in, and the front and rear windshields were spider's maze of crack's and splinters from impacts.

Dazed at first in disbelief, he scanned the car, looking for any eviudence to prove or disprove what he saw. As he walked over to the damaged side, he squinted into the interior, looking for any evidence, becoming his own technician looking for some information. When he peered through the window on the rear door, he saw it. The book. It had been tossed onto the back seat, and it now laid there before him. With small broken pieces of glass surrounding it like tiny diamonds, he knew for sure this was the car, and that Michael was here somewhere.

But there was now something else. Something deep inside began to stir, and he looked away from the sedan and gazed at the chaos all around him. Tarps were now covering the bodies and pieces they were finding. Bright red, they deliberately stood out amongst the darkness scattered around, but the scene was familiar to him the smell of burnt flesh and hair, the splattering of blood and entrails mixed with the disfigured items of a common household. The horrible fuzzy fog of smoke and steam from the water of the fireman's house put everything into a surreal light. A door to a different would of tragedy and confusion.

He had been here before, He know these smells and sights and sounds and they were around him again as if they had never left. Taunting him into remembering the horror; that particular horror.

Dresden, Germany in March of 1945 was idyllic./ At that time, spring was close, but so were the Allies. The war was beginning it's end game and despite 4 years of war, the centuries old city had been spared. Whereas other cities had been pounded into dust because of their strategic industrial and transportation centers, Dresden only offered the past. Medieval architecture graced by centuries old cathedrals and Gothic sculpture.

Joseph had just left home where his mother was scolding her two older sisters; one two years, the other three years older. He smiled as his mother's threats began to fill the house at their inattentiveness to their duties. He on the other hand was on his way to the piano teacher's residence about a half mile away for his thrice weekly lesson. Along the way he passed the shops and bakeries that defined their lives and added a charm to their home.

The years of rationing had closed many stores, and some of the residents he knew had few clothes remaining that weren't tattered and patched. Still, for a thirteen year old who had known little else, there was not much to compare it to. Having taken this path so many times, he knew many people by sight, and he was also familiar to them as they nodded a greeting as he walked by.

For some, he seemed an anomaly as there were few boys left of his age remaining in the town. Some were hiding in the hills; others who couldn't afford to leave were staying low in the city: rarely leaving the house. The vast majority were conscripted. Whereas he was holding sheets of music, they were shouldering anti-tank grenades and rifles. Many of the boys he knew, and to be around their families he could sense the emptiness and the uncertainty.

His excuse was his father's power. His father ran one of the mills and with few other able bodied men left, someone was needed to run the power plants and fix whatever could be fixed with what parts were available. As a young boy he was learning the mechanics of buildings and the fundamentals of power sourcing, yet with his mother's insistence he was also learning some culture along with his homeschooling. Hence, he was now walking up the three front stairs to the large wooden front door and rang the bell to alert the elderly lady within that he was here for his lesson.

Quickly the door opened and he was greeted curtly, with the disciplined immediacy of a teacher with an agenda. Reaching into his pocket, he dropped the coins for the lesson in a large glass bowl by the staircase, and then entered the spacious parlor. He placed the music on the stand, cracked his knuckles for effect, then began his scales as the teacher stood over him, watching his fingering and mentally calibrating the tempo.

He had just begun his second set, when the sirens went off. "Mien Gott!" she uttered then brushed him away from the piano, and the two of them scampered into the cellar under the stairs by the back door. As they descended down, he could feel the coolness of the earth surrounding him, drawing him into the secure chamber, where a single bare bulb lit up a small bench, some chairs, and a stack of books. Once situated in the cool earth of the basement, he realized he was now surrounded by shelves of jars and cans of provisions and a giant vat of water. They could stay down here for weeks if they had to, but every time the siren wailed, it quickly sounded the all clear soon after as the bombers were just passing over, heading towards other targets that were more important than their city.

But this was different. He could hear explosions as the bombs began to fall. Distant at first, they grew closer as the bombers finished their runs. Around them the earth began to shake as the concussions shook the ground. Near misses caused the dust to rise and when one of the storage shelves broke, sending a cascade of jars onto the floor, Josef jumped from his chair and into the willing arms of the Frau, shook just as violently from her fear of the bombs.

He prayed they would pass over, but the bombing lasted for hours. Endlessly the ground shook as more shelves tumbled, a chair fell over, and the stack of books was quickly laid flat. Josef held here for so long his fingers grew numb, yet the fear was constantly refreshed as the bombs cleared away the house above them, and struggled mightily to get at them.

The bombing continued for hours, and as he clung to her, he felt her shaking abate, and her limbs grow loose. As a wave of bombs grew close, he would scream to lessen the fear and ease the panic. Amongst the noise he could barely hear himself. The concussions seemed to knock his hearing back each time until it became a steady ringing.

With one last wave of bombs, he heard it recess, then fade, then they were gone. Around him the darkness prevailed, and the air was still thick with dust. Yet there was now silence. The last of the thuds had faded away. He let go of the woman, yet, she didn't seem to move to him. She just sat on the bench, quiet almost lifeless, as if her soul had unplugged, leaving only an empty vessel.

Carefully rising from the bench, he reached along the floor until he found a flashlight that had been knocked off its shelf. Clicking it on, he scanned the room, the light diffused by the dust. When he shown it on the music teacher, he stared intently at someone he no longer knew. Her skin was pale, her hair full of the dust from the floors above them, yet her eyes were small and dark, with the whites turned red from the unblinking intensity.

"Frau?.." he asked, his tone sounding distant from the damage to his lungs.

Slowly, she turned to look at him, her eyes squinting slightly to see, as if he was some object far in the distance.

"Frau…." He repeated. "Are you okay?" she then turned to look around her, but then quietly returned to looking into the empty foreground. The bombs had blown a large hole in her consciousness that now pulled everything into it, creating a dark void out of a functioning human being.

"I will go get help." He replied, then shown the light on the door above them. It was still solid, and when he went up to open it, it failed to budge from the warped frame. Scavenging in the basement, he was able to find a hammer and a metal bar with which to begin chiseling his way out.

For how long he worked, he wasn't sure. It could have been hours, or minutes, but eventually he was able to punch a hole through it. Still in darkness, he was able to shine the light through the hole and see all of the debris in his way. As luck would have it, the heavy beans from the upstairs had fallen must above the door itself, filling the space in front of him with only small debris, which he was able to loosen and pull through or push to the side.

Punching through a chunk of plaster wall about three feet past the doorway, the room was suddenly filled with an orange light.

"I'm through!" he exclaimed, and he turned back to the woman. Despite his efforts, she hadn't moved, she still sat there arms to her side, staring at the emptiness in front of her. "I'll get help." He exclaimed, then made the final leap through the hole and into the new landscape before him.

Whether it was dawn or dusk, he wasn't sure as everything around him was unfamiliar. Stout houses and thickly paved streets had been erased, and around him for miles was a charred and leveled landscape. What the bombs had destroyed the fires had burned until there was nothing but low, blackened slopes of ash and charred timber.

The entire city center stretched before him and he could see emptiness for miles. His home, his family the mill; everything had been erased. Struggling to breathe through the smoke and the thin oxygen, weakened by the phosphorous in the incendiaries, he tried to ascertain where his home would be. In a break in the smoke, he glimpsed the cathedral in the distance, crippled, but still standing. Wiping a tear away from his blackened face, he then began to climb over the debris towards the angel far in the distance, still perched on the high arch of the cathedral.

Michael stumbled out of the restaurant and into the debris field as nearby witnesses ran towards him and the wounded lying on the ground. Amongst the screams and moans of the wounded, his presence almost seemed to be ignored. Only a few people noticed him, and because he was conscious and upright, he didn't garner the same attention as the others. Walking between cars, and avoiding heavy throngs of people, he managed to get to the edge of the parking lot.

Suddenly confronted by three men, he heard the lead man speak in a muffled tone. Assuming they were asking if he was okay, he nodded. He was and waved them off toward the scene of the explosion where he was sure he they were need more. Running past him, Michael then looked around for a place to hide. Seeing some semi-trailers parked in a row out at the end of the strip mall, he headed in that direction. He wanted to run, but he was beginning to feel a tightening in his legs, almost a numbness that made walking suddenly a little difficult. Looking around it seemed that no one seemed to be any attention to him, and he strode the fifty yards or so over to them.

Looking back at the restaurant, he could see police cars pulling up and police officers running and bending over people on the ground. Certain he was in the clear, he darted between the trailers. Walking towards their back doors, he saw that they pushed up against a thick wall of brush that bordered a forest preserve. Using the length of the rear of the trailer, he tried to slip behind the rear wheels with the bed above him as cover now he could not be seen unless they were looking for him, and sitting awkwardly under the semi-trailer, he tried to stretch out his legs.

For the first time, he noticed how badly cut up he was, His pants were shredded in some spots, and he could see hundreds of small cuts and tears in the fabric as the shrapnel had sliced its way through the cloth an into his legs. Dark patches of blood had appeared, but were already drying as the blood was clotting. Looking down at his feet he saw his left sock full of blood, obviously running down his leg, but other than that, no serious injury.

With the dim of his ear adding a steady hum, he was reassured that there was no one looking for him. Now he had some time to consider what he should do. Slipping into a dull funk, he listened as in the distance sirens wailed and people yelled, while he closed his eyes, feeling the pain in his legs build and just concentrated on his heart beating steadily, one pound at a time.

How long he lay there, he was uncertain. The noise around him never seemed to change, and it seemed to reassure him that he could go back if he wanted to. A doctor, and ambulance, pain killers were just a few hundred yards away, yet he felt deep satisfaction at knowing he got away. He had escaped from the mess he was in, and here amidst the smell of exhaust and grease and rubber, he was secure. But now he had think – what now?

As if on cue, he heard the scratch of boots on gravel, He slowly turned his head and glared out at the pavement between the trailers. Not seeing anything, he once again heard the scratching, and then suddenly a worn pair of hiking boots attached to thickly calved jeans tucked into red and grey wool socks suddenly appeared. They kept shifting as their owner kept shifting from one trailer to another; looking. In a flash, they were gone, then suddenly reappearing, and Michael saw what the bots were so intensely tracking. Between them there was a small pool of blood. A clue that left from his shoe as he had struggled to crawl under the trailer.

For a second, there was a sudden feeling of relief that a decision has been made. No need for a plan, his discovery eliminated that. He watched as the shoes shuffled again reappeared, then a shoe slowly bend as the knee brought the man down to his lever. Suddenly, Michael was looking at a thick man in a flannel shirt buttoned to the top and tacked tightly into his jeans. Looking back at him was a round face with a two day stubble, thick rounded glasses, and thin lips. Taken aback slightly by the eyes enlarged by the lens, he was also curious about a black knit cap on his head, pulled tightly down beyond his ears such that it appeared as a skull cap.

He watched as his rescuer gazed at him, then his legs, then up at him again. He stood up again, looking back at the crime scene, then bent down again.

Michael now came to the conclusion that this was not a first responder, which brought the question again; Now what? Once again the stranger bent down and looked at his legs. This time he nodded and held out a thickly calloused hand. Reacting, Michael reached out with his own bloodied hand and allowed the stranger to pull him out from under the trailer. His legs had tightened up from the inactivity and any movement caused sharp barbs of pain, yet he was able to push himself out, then attempt to stand.

Leaning on the stranger, Michael and the man looked b ack at the carnage smoldering in the distance.

"I can't go back there." Michael blurted out.

The stranger grabbed Michael's arm, strung it over his shoulder an turned him around. With some effort, he was able to help Michael reach the narrow grassed strip a the end of the trailer. As in a long tall wall of greenery appeared before them, with old growth trees leaning over the, the stranger pulled Michael tighter, and then they plunged into the mass of leaves and branches, and disappeared.

CHAPTER II

J osef turned the latch and slowly pushed his front door
open. Turning, he waved halfheartedly at the car
pulling out of the driveway. In return the driver – Michael's
father – nodded and pulled away. He was headed back to
the house where all the relatives had begun to gather.
At the accident scene, Josef and Andrea had checked in
with the investigators and were informed that Michael
was not listed among the wounded or the dead, but they
would officially listed as missing due to the car. They
emphasized that confusion was a common factor after this
and he may have been taken to the hospital by a Good
Samaritan. As such, they were told to go home and wait
until notified.

In the car on the way back, phone calls were made,
the chain of communication had begun its work. Andrea's
mom, Josef's daughter, lived a thousand miles away, but
upon hearing the news, Josef was assured she would be
here within 24 hours. By the time they had returned home
to Andrea's house, Michael's parents were already there,
the neighbor that had babysat the kids had left to spread
the news of the tragedy, and the children were strangely

silent, knowing that something was dreadfully wrong, and dad wasn't home.

After spending all afternoon there, Josef asked for a lift home so he could wash up and rest. The stress had taken its toll and he was exhausted. He took the ride offered, with the promise to Andrea that he would collect a small bag and return later on his own, to spend the night.

Walking through the living room, he strode into the kitchen and opened the cabinet above the sink. Taking out a low, flat glass, he then reached into the cabinet by the refrigerator and grasped the bottle of brandy he kept as a reserve. Pouring a shot or two into the glass, he exhaled and swallowed half in a quick tip of the glass. The smoke was still in his nose from the fire, and with a natural shove, the liquor pushed it out, burning the smell from his sinuses and cutting through the blackened patch in the back of his throat.

Having had little to eat, he felt the lift of the alcohol right away, and the harsh edges of shock and grief began to soften. He left the bottle on the counter and walked towards the bedroom at the rear of the house, where his stacks of books awaited him. Walking amongst the stacks, he made his way to the plush chair next to a buried desk, where he did his reading, and fell into it with a heavy slide.

Scanning around him, he felt comforted by the written words around him, encased and bound, ready for his eyes. These books, these authors and artists were his friends, the companions he drew closer too upon the death of his wife, a few years earlier. Taking a few deep breaths, he took the last of the brandy in another gulp, then stared at the desk in front of him.

He knew what was there, and for the first time in a long while, he felt the need to visit the thin black case hidden deep in the depth of the lowest drawer below the writing surface. Waiting until the rush set in, he then rose, opened the drawer and reached behind a stack of business papers. Feeling it's soft velvet surface, he grasped it, then set back down in the chair. He opened the worn velvet jewelry case, the hinge creaking with age and rust. In the palm of his hand, in a nest of cotton, was an old skeleton key, a melted spoon, and a small brown clasp envelope holding yellowed teeth.

As as child, when he had found his way back to his home after the bombing, he shuffled through the ash and cracked brick, looking for anything from his family, finding only these three artifacts to attest to where a family had once been. He remembered holding them tight in his hands, sleeping in the rubble for few days, until the soldiers appeared, fed him, and moved him to a small camp where many newly orphaned children were collected.

Despite all his travels and suffering; the countless hours and barracks he shuffled towards and through, he always holding the small treasures as holy relics, signposts to his past. He now gazed at them, held the cool metal in his hands, the roughness of the root of the tooth in his palm, he glanced at the soot and ash smudged into his shirt and pants and once again felt close to that history.

When he had satisfied the pull of his heart, and validated his memories, he replaced the articles into the box with the exception of the spoon. He then closed the box with a snap and placed it back into its hiding place.

He placed the spoon in his palm of his hand and closed it into a fist. The cool metal began to warm from his shin, and in his and he could imagine his past coming alive with it. He seemed closer somehow, as if he could bring the past forward and it could suddenly appear all around him, pulling him back such that he could experience again what was now gone. Having pulled all the energy he could from it, he opened his fist and looked fondly at the twisted piece of metal, charred and melted and now rapidly cooling in his palm. Rising from his chair, he went back to the kitchen, and poured another shot of brandy, He then set the spoon on the kitchen counter, replaced the bottle, then walked into the bathroom to take a shower. In his mind he was already listing the clothes and sundries he would need while staying at Andre's house for the next few days.

Michael and his rescuer crashed through the border of buckthorn and after a rough approach, entered into a serene, silent landscape of forested undergrowth. Struggling at first to adjust to the man's strong strides, Michael did his best to keep up. Initially there were abundant cups and discarded plastic bags and other trash that had successfully run the gauntlet of crossing branches and thorns, but these faded quickly to the vines, ferns, and shade perennials. Michael could feel the moistness of the scene, yet the ringing in his ears seemingly amplified the silence of the woods.

Following a thin beaten path through the woods, barely wide enough to accommodate one man, let alone two, Michael struggled to keep up, almost falling a number of times into his rescuer when they approached tangles of tree roots and fallen branches. Sensing the difficulty, the man slowed his gait, shifting more of Michael's weight onto himself. With the adjustment, he was able to step cautiously in keeping up, yet, with his arm over his rescuers shoulder, he could hear the heavy breathing and feel the sweat seeping through the man's thick shirt.

After some time, they rested. The two of them finding a spot on a large fallen tree, tall enough so they didn't have to bend too far. For a second, Michael just panted, focused on controlling the pain in his legs with little regard to his escort. Closing his eyes to try and block out the ringing.

"Are you going to take me to the hospital?" He suddenly blurted out.

"Better." Was the response in an unusually soft voice.

"I think I should go to the hospital." He stated more strongly.

"If you wanted to go to the hospital, why were you hiding under the trailer?"

Before he could answer, Michael felt his arm lifted up and his weight lifted off his legs completely. Draping the young man over his back, he folded his charge's arms over his shoulders to use his frame as a pack animal.

Feeling uncomfortable, yet, out of pain, he didn't resist as they once again resumed the journey. He wasn't sure but Michael seemed to feel as if they were now moving faster, with him being carried versus dragged.

Occasionally looking ahead of them, he could see the trees becoming thicker and taller, with their all-encompassing canopies shielding the smaller thinner trees trying to establish. With breaks in the branches, beams of sunlight would reach down to the ground becoming strong pillars of light in the increasing darkness of the forest.

At first he could feel them gradually climbing as if they were approaching a low hill. Suddenly, he felt them descending sharply down the other side. The path now snaked slightly to prevent an out of control fall and to aid in the descent, the moist ground thick with moss.

The throbbing in his legs now began to overcome the ringing in his ears and he closed his eyes again to try and beat back the pain. An odd smell now began to ease into his nostrils. A wild smell; smoky but whether still in his nose from the smoke of the fire or a new smell drifting through the woods.

When it became very strong, Michael opened his eyes and as if on cue, his human mule halted. Before him lay one of the most unusual sights he had ever seen.

He was on the edge of a small village, consisting of a half dozen small cone shaped huts, each constructed from small saplings tied together with vines. Spaced evenly at the base of a hut, vines had been planted and allowed to grow over the top to create a green camouflage which blended in perfectly with the surrounding landscape. A few small fires were scattered around the open area in the center, and the ground had been stamped down hard from the constant foot traffic. By looking around him, this encampment appeared to have been here for some time.

After being set down on a stump, he awkwardly stretched out his legs, now stiff from inactivity. The blood had dried on his pants, creating red mosaic blotches on the fabric, now dried and hard.

"I will get you some water." His consort said and then trotted off towards one of the huts.

Sitting there at an uncomfortable angle, he felt dazed and weak. Through suddenly tired eyes, he looked back at a small collection of people standing in the green, open space, staring at him. None approached, nor did he encourage them too. In the distance, behind the others, he could see an old man suddenly appear out of one of the huts, he wore a open brown tunic, a thin black sweater underneath with thick paratrooper pants. His shaved head made his thick eyebrows and the large facial features seem ever more pronounced and as he walked towards the center, his eyes seemed only focused on him. Michael tried to stare back, but couldn't maintain the connection. His eyes instead dropping to stare at the clean white satchel he held in his hand.

Surprised by a sudden hand on his shoulder, Michael turned to see a water bottle thrust in his face. As if needing more prompting, his companion cracked the seal and removed the cap. Michael looked up and saw his rescuer's, soft blue eyes behind the thick glasses looking at him intently.

With a nod, Michael took the bottle with a bloodied hand, tipped it at the man in acknowledgement, and quickly drained it. Whatever it was; the loss of blood, smoke, the exertion or all of the above combined, the water was cold and clean and he suddenly craved it with a primal urge.

Finishing the bottle, he held it up, and it was instantly replaced with another container. Finishing half of the plastic bottle, he pulled it away and hesitated. Suddenly the water felt like a knot in his stomach and he had to pause to see if it was going to come back up. Oddly, the remaining water in the bottle began to slosh and he realized that both of his hands were shaking.

"That's just the shock setting in." The bald man exclaimed, having now reached him. Kneeling, down in front of his legs, the man opened up his bag and revealed a varied array of bandages, swabs, tape and ointments. Pulling out a small black valise hidden in a side pocket, he unzipped the three sides and opened it like a book. Inside it, were gleaming needles and tiny bundles of thread.

Whipping out pair of angled clinical scissors, he began to cut away the right leg of the trousers from the cuff up, once he was mid-thigh, he switched to the other leg, completely at the same spot.

"This is Dr. Coda," his compatriot started, "He's a real doctor." He added as if to validate the title of his first statement.

The man at his feet glanced up at him with dark eyes. "I will present my credentials upon request." He said in a smooth baritone. Then smiled at his own joke.

Reaching his mid-thigh, the doctor stopped, placed the scissors gently back into the bag, then slowly pulled the fabric away from the leg. As ugly as the pants were from the outside, the skin underneath looked like something pulled from the bottom of a lake. There was little of his skin that looked like his own. Cuts and slashes of every size and depth had scarred his leg and what wasn't bloody had already begun to bruise with a variety of blue, black and green colors.

The doctor nodded, then looked at the rescuer. "We need to get him into one of the huts so I can get started. He needs to be comfortable because this will take a while." He then looked at Michael sternly, like a teacher scolding a truant child. "You're lucky." He added in a surprisingly loud voice. "At least nothing hit an artery."

While the doctor slipped under the left shoulder, the other man took away his water and slipped under the right shoulder. Lifting him up, they carried him into the nearest shelter and closed the flap behind them.

Michael felt an immediate distinction between the cool summer air and the sudden staleness of the inside of the shelter. He could smell the humidity, like being in a crowded elevator on a hot day. He could also sense the sweetness of incense and the density of smoke.

They placed him on a blanket of mats and sleeping bags, then Dr. Coda removed the rest of his pants and began the work of cleaning the wounds. His assistant slipped out of the tent, then returned quickly with 4, gallon jugs of water along with a bundle of rags under his arm.

Lying flat on the mat, Michael suddenly became limp from exhaustion. He slipped into a light doze, as the coolness of the water on his legs as they were cleaned and massaged.

"I'm going to inject you with some pain killer." He heard the doctor say. In response he only grunted, but winced twice as the needle went into both legs. He slowly began to drift again, rousing occasionally as he felt the tug of the needle as the stitches went in.

When the doctor had finished, he opened his eyes slightly and watched as the doctor rose, reached over to a stack of blankets by the front door, and covered him.

"I'm all done," he said, "just get some rest."

Then he left, the flap closing behind him. In the brief time the flap was open, Michael could hear deep voices he couldn't recognize.

"Where did you find him?" a muttered reply.

"Why did you bring him here?"

"He's perfect for us." Was the answer. Then he slipped into a deep sleep.

Josef stared at the tv screen from his armchair, arms crossed, his thumb over his lips in deep thought.

"Our top story tonight; technicians have almost finished going through the remains of Antonios Pizzeria on 87th Street. Six people are now confirmed dead with thirty-seven wounded, twelve severely with burns and internal injuries caused by flying debris. At least three bodies were identified through DNA today as being Salvador Perez - 28, Bobby Wirley – 18, and Michael

Planck -24. The families have been notified and as of yet, there is no comment."

Josef clicked off the tv and sat for a while in the darkness. All the occupants were now asleep, the kids with lullabies, the mom with Ambien. Michael's parents had returned home with the vow of coming back in the morning.

After some time, he felt the need to turn on the light at the end table next to him, and after concentrated effort he reached over and clicked on the switch. With a snap, it revealed a soft white light which illuminated the living room. It seemed to bring noise and function to the room and he gazed around at the still toys, empty pizza boxes and blackened television screen.

His gaze settled on a white plastic packet laying on the table in the kitchen. The police had dropped it by earlier with their findings and their condolences. Contained within it was all the evidence they had that Michael was dead; the torn legging of a trouser, a wallet, and a mangled shoe. It lay on the table as a testament. The final chapter and the sadness it brought no one wanted to touch or even acknowledge was here. It seemed to Josef like as if it was a stray dog. Something no one wanted to call or attract or take care of, just something to walk around.

Josef rose and walked over to the table staring down at the packet, he slowly placed his hand on the cold plastic, trying somehow to be closer to it. He remembered again the scenes after the bombing. Survivors looking for anything of value in the rubble. What the bombs hadn't destroyed, the incendiaries had vaporized and melted into nothing but clumps and char. There wasn't even any water in the fountains because the extreme heat had boiled away the water, while in the far distance, he could see the railroad cars full of corpses, ready to be sent out to the county for burial.

'The small bits of artifacts were all that we had to link us to the past', he thought. When there was nothing, to hug or kiss or hold onto, one just grabs whatever he could find to remember.

With his other hand, he slipped it into his pants leg, feeling the coolness of the spoon's metal on his fingers; a touchstone to the past, as the images of his family slowly faded in and drifted out. He was sad not for himself, but for the children because he knew what the children had lost.

Turning away from the table, he returned to the living room and stretched out on the couch, tossing away one of the stuffed bug aliens stuck between the cushions. Reaching up, he clicked off the light and settled the pillows beneath his head, trying to find some comfort for his old bones. Finally getting stable, he didn't attempt to sleep, but rather stared out the patio doors at a full yellow moon wedged between two of the houses, it's ascendancy just beginning.

In a house not too far away, in the lowest level of a three tier basement designed to hide the opulence his operations had brought, a man in his forties took aim at a yellow billiard ball near a corner pocket. The gold chains around his neck lay on the mahogany bumper as he bent over as far as he could to aim his shot. Slowly he brought the diamond encrusted cue back, then slowly forward, then slowly back again, hesitating. With his arms fully stretched out the tattoos and etchings of a panther, unicorns and angels seemed to be a bleacher full of spectators at the sport. His hard brown eyes didn't blink as he calculated the distance, arch, and velocity; measurements needed to place the ball in the pocket.

With his concentration focused on the shot, he was oblivious to the suited man walking into the room with an I-Pad. Sliding against the wall as if to incorporate himself into the design of the wallpaper, he patiently awaited the shot with his shoulders back and his ringed hands folded over the computer.

With a quick thrust and a sharp crack, the stick struck the ball. In a white blur it streaked across the velvet, striking the target squarely, sending the '1' into the corner pocket with the same velocity, shuffling the others as if they were searching for cover like sheep before the wolf. In small clumps they reformed, with the exception of the striped '12' which drifted towards the side pocket alone. As planned, the cue ball set up three feet from its new target, allowing for another clean shot into the side pocket.

Raising his cue, the shooter extended his full height of six foot-four, his long sleeves sliding over his arms, allowing his barbaric tattoos to hide behind clean white linen. With unfocused attention, he reached out for the chalk, slowly grinding it over the tip as he watched the drama on the velvet. When the balls had settled, he nodded approvingly as the cue ball rolled and stopped within the desired distance.

He then looked over at the attendant, while taking the chalk and sliding it over the connecting tissue between his setting thumb and first finger. "How was collections?" has asked in a steady baritone.

"Got them all except one." was the reply. "Planck's dead." As proof, he extended the I-Pad out with an article listing the dead from the explosion listed prominently. He set it on the bumper in front of his boss, and then stepped back obediently.

Staring blankly at the article, returning to grind the chalk on the tip again, he replied." How much is he in to us for?"

"Fifteen Thousand.'

He grimaced, then stopped, motionless, for a few moments, staring at the article. Then he moved around the table to line up the next shot. Bending over his tattooed arms sliding out of the sleeves like fangs, he placed his hand out on the velvet, then slid the stick to draw up the shot. Silently, he drew the line, teasing the stick a few times to center the contact point, then abruptly stopping, and standing again.

"Look into that." He looked over at the I-Pad, then over to the attendant. "I have a feeling something is wrong. People who owe us money don't disappear unless they want to."

The attendant nodded, then snatched up and turned to leave.

"Use our connections at the station. I would spend a

few thousand to find him, if nothing more than to send a message." Quietly, the messenger slipped away, as the ivory balls cracked violently behind him.

For Andrea and the kids, the days blurred together. Sleep was intermittent and incomplete, possible only between pillars of grief and confusion. The children were young enough that now that the initial shock had worn off, they began playing again. Keeping them busy was her number one objective, easy to do as the neighbors swarmed around them, doing whatever they could do to ease the pain.

The package from the police that was dropped off lay on the table for a few days. Flowers and trays of food began to pile around it, really just another object to work around, but Andrea knew it was there, and glanced at it as she walked through on her way to somewhere else.

Finally, one afternnon when the kids were at a neighbors playing, she stopped and stood before the package. Staring at it as if it was a religious relic, she slowly lifted it up, and carried it as if it were a tray into her bedroom. Laying it on the bed, she closed the door and then sat next to it, apprehensive, as if it would suddenly speak to her.

On the end, the flap was closed and attached only with adhesive. It was easy to pull it open, and when she did, the room suddenly filled with the acrid smell of smoke and burnt plastic. Rather than reach in, she slowly turned the envelope upside down, letting the contents tumble onto the comforter. Setting the envelope off to the side, she stared at the small pile in front of her.

Her silent witness only consisted of a shredded pant leg, blackened and torn from the force of the explosion. There was one shoe, equally torn, and a wallet in remarkably good condition. She separated the pants leg from the others, placing it back in the bag, her nose beginning to run either from the grief returning or the aggravation of the smell. Picking up the wallet it popped open and she smiled at his picture on the license. Thumbing through the credit cards, she saw and then pulled out a dog-eared picture of her and the kids taken six months ago. She smiled at the small family smiling back at her, wiping away a tear sliding down her cheek. Carefully she placed it back - folded, the wallet closed, then placed it back on the night stand, by where he slept.

Taking up the shoe, the last remaining item, she held it cupped in her hands, the last article documenting his existence. She gazed at it, the leather discolored, laces incinerated, and the stitching scorched. She didn't recognize it as his, yet she cherished it as if he had just taken it off. Slowly she stood up and carried it over to where all of his other shoes had been, neatly arranged on the floor of the closet. She placed it in an open space on the end, in perfect alignment with the others, like boats at a dock, only this one was forlorn and misshapen.

The crying came again, and the pain radiated through her chest as she worked through the emotion. How long she sat there she didn't know, the emotion took time to work through, and when it had, she stared at the open closet in front of her.

But as she stared at the shoes, something felt odd. Wrong. She stared at the misfit shoe in relation to the others, and stared, and stared. Finally, she reached down and picked it up again. Next, she picked up another shoe from the same foot. She placed the heels together, then slowly rolled the soles together, till they ended up placed together at the tip. With astonishment, the damaged shoe was two inches shorter than Michaels.

Throwing the shoe to the side, she did it again with another, then another, all of them larger than the damaged shoe she held in her hand. Elation suddenly filled her chest, when she realized that he could be alive, maybe unconscious somewhere, or wandering aimlessly in the streets. But then she began to think; the wallet by the leg, the missing cousin, no cell phone, all the other victims accounted for, the wallet again – undamaged and clean, as if it had just been tossed in the pile.

Then a darkness began to come over her. She felt it in the back of her head, and as it moved forward, her scalp tightened, her cheeks flushed and her eyes grew narrow. "The son-of-a-bitch is still alive." She whispered hoarsely under her breath as she reached for the business card on the bed.

CHAPTER III

M ichael woke up with a start. Wide eyed, he looked around him at an odd environment where nothing looked familiar, yet seemed comforting. Above him, the young trees bent over and tied for support became, seemed surprisingly reassuring. The dried thatch of twigs and evergreen branches were entwined in a thick layer, allowing for a dense cover against the rain and snow and he followed their pattern as he rose to full consciousness.

Feeling stronger, he raised his head so he could look over the opened sleeping bags layered over him for blankets. He saw the mountains of pillows and cushions around him, some scattered singularly, other piled into mounds along the sides. He glanced at the blanket used as a front door, then at the floor made from a weave of some dark, heavy fiber, possibly reeds.

He looked at either side, noting empty bowls with spoons, and a clear vase of water, which triggered a sudden thirst. Turning to reach for the vase he felt a stiffness in his torso and arms a soreness not from injury, but from inactivity. Reaching the vase he gulped down half the contents quickly, pausing to collect his breath before finishing the last of the water.

Placing the empty vessel next to him, he returned to laying down and staring at the natural weave laced above him. Flipping through his memory, he was able to pull together some collective thoughts of staying in the hut, the stranger who stitched his legs, another dark figure with a deep voice. As the thoughts grew stronger, his breathing grew deeper, and his muscles began to feel the need to move. He pulled the sleeping bag back, stretching his arms out, feeling the sharp ping of inactivity replaced very quickly with a warmth as the blood rushed into shallow veins and arteries, and blood reached and heated up distant muscles that had tightened up from laying down too long.

Feeling the motion returning to his arm, he pushed himself up to his elbows. Before him was his bare legs, graced only with the prescence of his boxer shorts. He inhaled sharply at the gruesome skin before him. Almost his entire skin was covered in bruises graced with blue and black and green blotches. Intermittently there were small thatches of twine, like thatches of brush on a barren landscape.

Slowly he tried to move his legs. He saw his thighs tighten, his toes twitch, and his knees turn as the legs began to move. The first wave of pain surprised him with its ferocity and he gulped and let out a sharp scream at the same time. As if on cue, the doctor burst through the front flap, a look of astonishment, quickly turning to concern as he examined the patient in front of him.

"Try not to move so suddenly.' He remarked.

Michael nodded, still unsure of how to react, or what to say. He lowered his knee down to the ground again, as the doctor kneeled next to him, put on a pair of round glasses from this pocket, and leaned over the pair of legs in front of him that had been his project over the last few days.

"If you move too quickly, you might pop the stitches. Convinced with his cursory exam, that everything was intact, he moved the glasses to the top of his head and looked directly at Michael, placing his hands flatly on his knees.

"How are you feeling?" He asked softly

Michael crossed his brow as he thought intently. "Sore." was his first response. "some pain when I move."

The doctor nodded. "there is a salve that I want you to put on your legs. It will ease the pain and at the same time medicate the wounds so they won't get infected." As he spoke he took out a wide mouth jar that he had hidden in his cloak. The glass was clear and Michael could see a thick grayish substance the consistency of bacon grease through the glass.   "This will also loosen the skin so it isn't so tight around the stitches, making it easier to move around." While he was talking, he unscrewed the jar, and this horrid stench wafted out of the container. Michael immediately felt his stomach clench, blood racing to it to expel the water already nestled within.

"God!! That smells terrible!" he yelled. "It smells like wet dog!"

"Once the salve is applied, the smell goes away. It just smells bad now because it has been in this jar so long."

Michael stared at the jar, then stared at the doctor kneeling before him, which suddenly opened the door to all sorts of questions.

"Who are you?" Michael asked defensively.

"I am Dr. Coda, and to anticipate your next few questions; I am a real doctor, with a degree; you are in a friendly commune deep in the woods; and right now you cannot go anywhere until your legs heal; so get comfortable. There will be someone outside the door if you need something so don't be afraid to shout."

Michael exhaled loudly, then laid down flat, looking at the ceiling. He swallowed hard, and looked at his caretaker once again. With a weak smile, the Dr. presented the open jar, nudging in it towards him, then placed it next to him.

"Be sure to shout if you need anything." He said as he rose up. "Ok, and if you get bored, there are some books you can read in a stack just above your head. Rest comfortably." And with a flip of the canvass, he was out of the structure.

Michael rose again on his elbows and turned his torso so he could see a small stack of 8 to 10 hardcover books. He exhaled deeply. "Books again."

Josef and Andrea sat on the couch, the package on the low table in front of them with the detective seated across from them. Leaning forward detective Bateman stared at the evidence, then looked again at her.

"So you're saying these are not your husband's clothes?"

"No their not. The shoes are too small and that is not the pants he was wearing when he left."

"But this matches the description you left, the clothes are a match, and so are the shoes. We found his wallet next to them at the scene of the explosion." He leaned back, gazed at Josef for a hope of some support, and seeing none, turned his attention back to the articles in front of him. "Miss," he began "when something this tragic happens, it is easy to search for and latch onto hope, any hope, even something that seems........" he thought carefully. "reasonable."

"Look." She interjected. "his is my husband's tennis shoe," and as if by magic pulled a shoe out from under the coffee table. Setting it down next to the shoe on the table, she presented her evidence. "It is much larger than the one you brought to me. These pants are the right color, but the wrong style and it's cheap." She pulled at the fabric as if to test it. "My husband would never wear this."

"Are you sure?"

She crossed her arms in indignation. "I buy my husband's clothes, because he is incapable of dressing himself. If left to his own decision, he would wear a Hawaiian shirt with sweatpants only because they are clean. Hell, he thinks grey is a color."

Detective Bateman pursed his lips and sat back in the sofa. Frustrated at having a closed case suddenly burst open again. "I see." Was all he could say.

At the peak of the stand off, her cell phone rang resting quietly on the arm of the sofa rang, she glanced at the number. "I have to take this." She said as she rose, pushed her hair back, and walked towards the kitchen.

Josef gave her an inquisitive glance, whereupon she answered. "It's Cecilia." He nodded in acknowledgement.

"Who's Cecilia?" The detective asked in a low voice.

"Michael's cousin." Josef answered. "His other cousin Riley has been reported missing and everyone is looking for him. No sign of him so far.

"Really." The detective blurted out, then paused. "What's his name again?" as he took out a pad of paper and a pencil.

On the third day, Michael awoke with a start, After days of battling fatigue and pain, he suddenly felt alive. He stretched his arm, tightened his thighs and wiggled his ties, feeling discomfort but not the pain. His strength was back, the pain was all but gone, he felt alive and ready to go.

Shifting, slightly, he snapped up to his elbows, flung the covers off of him and stared down at the pair of legs underneath him, now looking more like a pair of legs instead of two meat sticks.

In preparation, a new pair of pants and shirt lay folded next to him, dropped off as he slept, by one of his phantom attendants. Bending over, he slipped the pants over his feet, when the waist band reached his knees, he slowly, cautiously bent his knees and then slipped them over. Rolling to one side, he pulled it up to his waist, felt some of the stitches ache after being sensitive to the fabric, yet it was a feeling that was quickly forgotten.

Snapping the button and pulling the zipper into place, he then shrugged off the t-shirt, tossing it into a mass of pillows, and shipped on the blue buttoned flannel shirt he was given.

He glanced around for shoes, his socks were still not on his feet; and not seeing any, decided to just go out and risk it. Struggling, he managed to reach a standing position, and is looking around from the perspective, realized how small this hut really was. Half walking, half shuffling, he reached the entrance, flinging the blanket back, and stepped to the outside.

He remembered the scene around him where he first arrived vaguely. Now the details were apparent, the bigger picture he first experienced flushed out. He could see about eight more huts similar to his, with a few small campfires with tripod cooking pots over them. There were a few people walking around, dressed for the outside in thick shirts, heavy boots and dirty jeans. The ground around him was packed hard from the traffic, with the sharp distinction between where the village ended and the forest being abrupt. It was always vigilant and close waiting patiently for the opportunity to retake what some had acquired. With the swatches of branches and leaves, and the tree branches towering overhead, creating a shaded density and a closeness. It all reminded him of the Native American village dioramas he had made in school, only instead of indian figures, there were now modern weekend suburbanites.

What amazed him was the sounds. There were none. People tended to talking hushed tones, there were no animals or children. so that dynamic was gone, and with the exception of only a few clusters of people, there was little interaction of any kind. Just people in a village going about a normal day, tending to their duties. Less drama, more routine. What he didn't see was the doctor coming up behind him and putting his hand on Michael's shoulder.

"You're feeling better." He stated with an expressionless look.

"Yea, yea." Michael agreed. "Where am I?" he asked. "Is this some sort of weird campout."

"No." the doctor said, and he turned to look at the scene around him, the same that Michael was trying to take in.

"No, not camping, this is just a place to stay while recuperating. More of a weigh station where people can come to rebuild their strength and reconnect with what's important."

"Oh, he replied." So these people came here for a vacation."

"Well, they don't come here because they want to. We find them, and show them an open door so to speak."

"How long do they stay?'

"They are only allowed to stay 10 weeks, then they have to leave."

"What if they don't want to leave?'

"Trust me, they are ready to leave, and none have ever needed to return. "Look," the doctor added, "there is someone you need to meet; Also, we need to get you some shoes. Luckily for you the 'The Mule' will be here tomorrow."

As he motioned with his arm to a hut at the far end of the enclosure, the cloak fell away and Michael saw a complex tattoo on his forearm. It was a green band, with an arrow and a two above it pointing to a red band. From the red band, there is an arrow with a five above it, pointing to a black band.

Before he could ask, the doctor began to walk away at a quick pace, with his arm now deeply buried in his sleeves. Obediently Michael followed his guide as they walked passed sullen individuals going about the simple tasks of housekeeping in the village; stoking fires, repairing clothing, preparing food. Occasionally Dr. coda would raise his hand in recognition, with that person returning it with a nod or a responding hand.

Surprisingly to Michael, not one seemed to notice his presence with nothing more knowing than a passing glance or a hesitation in their work. He also noticed everyone was dressed in current clothing, or if they had just walked off the street as he had. No pretense of living a better life through subsistence living here, just ordinary people living in the woods.

With difficulty, he struggled to keep up in his bare fee, the Dr. continuing at his own pace. Soon, he had progressed 10 yards or so ahead. Too bashful to ask him to slow down he struggled in his bare feet, wincing at the sharp stones and twigs he was stepping on. The muscles in his legs, weak from inactivity, now demanded that he stop moving, having become soft from laying dow, they wanted to shut down from the demands of the brain, sending sharp, painful messages to frontal cortex, warning of an immediate collapse. Suddenly, at the end of the walk, Dr. Coda stopped and stepped aside. Suddenly rising before him was a hut. Similar to the on he had left, which made it the same design as all the others, only twice the size, with an equally wider door. Following the lead presented by the doctor, Michael caught up and pushed aside the curtained doorway and into a large, mostly empty room with less pillows, more light from clear plastic in pockets of the roof, and a lot more carpet.

In the center was three directors chairs, facing each other in a small circle. The two on his right and left were empty, but seated in the one in the center was a tall, thin, dark skinned man, with his receding black hair tied into dreadlocks, and those pulled together in the back and held together with a thin leather strap. Hs long jaw was speckled with a closely shaved beard. His eyes were what caught Michaels attention in that they were an ultra-light brown and with the pupils seemingly extra large, he seemed animated, almost reptilian in his presentation. Seated with his legs and arms crossed, the man looked up at Michael suddenly and smiled pleasantly unfolding his arms and lacing his fingers together, resting them on his lap.

"Good morning." He said softly. "Welcome. How are you?"

"Better." Michael replied as he and Dr. Coda sat down in the chairs facing him.

"Dr. Coda says that you should have a full recovery, given that you have had a sufficient amount of rest." The Dr. nodded in compliance. "Now." The gentleman said as he unfolded his legs and placed his hands flat on his knees. "I'm sure you have plenty of questions." What would you like to know?"

"Where am I? What is this place? Some sort of commune?"

The facilitator hesitated and thought carefully. "This is not a commune or any type of organized long term community. There are some full time people here like myself and Dr. Coda, but everyone else here is only here for a ten week period. No longer." He raised his finger to make this point. "Anyone, however, can leave whenever they wish. There is no requirement to stay."

"So it is like summer camp?'

He thought again. "It is a refuge for people who need to ...... hesitate in their life."

Michael paused as he took this in.

"No one here is suffering from addictions, financial distress, abuse or hiding from the authorities. Which brings me to my first question. Have you broken the law?"

Michael responded surprisingly quickly. "No."

Everyone nodded. "Good, does that answer your first question?"

"Yes."

"Do you have another?"

"Yes, who are you?'

"My name is Hayden Piedmont and my job here........ is to listen."

"That sounds easy."

"It can be."

"So everyone comes here just to talk?"

"Well, we find them and as in your situation, if we think there is some virtue that we can draw out and develop, we allow them to stay."

"So I was recruited?"

"Somewhat. Our field associate saw you come out of the restaurant and instead of pursing aid with the authorities, you willingly ran away and hid."

"Well, you see…" Michael began.

Hayden held up a flattened palm. "Not now." He said, stopping Michael. "Later."

As if on cue, the war sweet smell of cooking meat began to waft through the curtained doorway. Michael's stomach suddenly clenched and he wiped the corners of his mouth as the salvia began to flow.

"That smells good."

"Let's get you something to eat." Dr. Coda said while giving Michael a studied look. "It's been a few days with no solid food." The Dr. was rising, when he was stopped midmotion by Hayden's hand on his shoulder.

"Let's put him with Mr. Wong tomorrow." He said to Dr. Coda's nod. He then turned to Michael and smiled pleasantly. "It was nice to meet you. We will meet again tomorrow."

"When?"

Mr. Piedmont shrugged and smiled, as Dr. Coda touched Michaels's elbow to encourage him to rise and follow him out of the shelter, which Michael did hungrily.

"Good evening and welcome to the KTAC six o'clock news. In a followup story to the explosion of the Mexican restaurant in the Starlite shopping mall, it has been determined that one of the victims was misidentified. One of the victims was listed as Michael Planck, it has now been determined that the correct name of the victim was Riley Ortment, a man in his late twenties who had just moved to the area."

"In a cruel twist of fate, Mr. Ortment is a cousin of Mr. Planck's. Detectives had said there are no leads in the case and there is some speculation that he may have survived the explosion and may be in the vicinity. Mr. Planck is 5' 11", 190 lbs., with brown hair and no facial hair. He was wearing beige shorts with a green polo shirt. If anyone has seen this individual, please call local authorities right away as he may be needing medical attention."

"In a breaking story, the son of a local appliance store owner has reported that his sixteen year old is missing. He was reported as not coming home after school yesterday. He was reported as being on the bus after school was dismissed, but disappeared sometime between being dropped off at his stop, and his home….."

The tv was clicked off in the billiard room, and for a few moments quiet hung like a mist throughout the room. The newscast had stopped the action with the gravity of the immediate story, and the validation of a theory.

"You were right chief. He is still alive."

But the boss wasn't listening. He was staring at the vacant screen, his mind planning silently, coolly, piecing together details and facts and working them into conclusions and eventually actions.

"Our contact at the station, what's his take on the missing client?"

"Unknown, they are starting to search, but they are two days behind. He promises they will find him, but it will take awhile."

He nodded, "What about the boy??" Wasn't it clear that the police wouldn't be notified?"

"Yes sir." Replied a very nervous associate situate along the wall behind him. "But the client said it was his ex-wife and she didn't quite grasp what was going on."

He nodded slowly again, this time his jaw working feverously. Quietly everyone waited for what they knew was coming.

Suddenly, he took the pool cue from the table and crashed it against the bumper, snapping it in half. With the butt in his hand, he marched out of the room, with his entourage following slowly behind.

Rapidly going down two flights of stairs, he then reached the utility door at the end and kicked the opening bar fiercely, causing the metal door to slam against the concrete wall.

With his arms stiff with anger, he strode over to the boy tied to an aluminum chair, his mouth taped shut. The attendant looked over his magazine as his boss marched into the room. He didn't move as the man walked over in front of the boy, stood squarely over him and looked down on a brave, withery face. In a fluid motion the blunt end of the cue struck the boy on the side of his left eye, with the back swing crushing the bridge of the victim's nose. Blood flowed out like a river over the grey duct tap on his mouth and he struggled to breathe, choking on his own blood.

Ripping the tape off of his mouth, the boy gulped in air between sobs, tears streaming from his right eye while this left swelled up, almost closing.

The boss bent down in front of him, inches from his face.

"Now we're going to make a video. In it you're going to tell our dad to shut the fuck up, or he'll get you back in installments, just like one of his refrigerators. Understand??

The boy nodded sharply.

"Good." He then rose and went to the closest associate. "Get it done and sent to the old man, use the boy's phone so ours aren't traced and send it from the park so the towers don't get this location."

Much more calmly the boss strode back through the utility door, his footsteps echoing on the concrete stairs. "I'm hungry." He yelled as he progressed back up to the main level.

Michel was escorted to a fire pit where a metal kettle had been set up. A low fire had kept it going, and the Dr. took the ladle and pulled up a soup spoon of steaming stew, which he poured into a wooden bowl which he received from a stack by the fire. When it was ¾ full, Michael was handed the bowl and a wooden spoon, which the Dr. had seemingly pulled from somewhere, and he then motioned for him to indulge.

"Take what you want." The Dr. said. "There is always

food here and you can eat as much as you want, anytime you like."

Michal gazed down at the bowl filled with small chunks of meat, green peppers, and potatoes. All fitting neatly into a rich gravy. "What is this?" he asked, his curiosity causing only a brief hesitation, with his hunger winning out as he brought a spoonful to his mouth, casually blowing on it to cool it off.

The Dr. shrugged. "Vegetables and herbs we've grown here, flour and sugar we've acquired, meat we have lucked into."

Michael hesitated, looking warily at the Dr. Coda. Sensing his trepidation, the Dr. smiled weakly.

"We don't hunt." He replied. "That was a deer killed by a truck recently and we acquired it before it was dragged away by someone else."

With the explanation acceptable, Michael took a small bite, followed by a gulp as he swallowed the entire contents of the spoon. The taste was amazingly good, fitfully enhanced by his hunger as he rapidly consumed the bowl, and edged towards the pot to fill it again.

"Since you are eating well," the Dr. advanced, I need to attend to a few items, please feel free to eat what you like and if you feel up to it walk around the camp." With a sudden flap of his coat, the Dr. rose and disappeared amongst the huts.

Michael was too focused on eating to really pay attention to what was going on around him. After the third bowl, however, he began to slow down and take stock of what is actually around him. What initially seemed to be a pagan village on the edge of civilization now really appeared to be a modern version of a Renaissance village, with attendants maintaining roofs, cleaning out and sweeping huts, bringing bundles of wood to the fire, and the basic housekeeping any community would need to do.

The people seemed to be no different than anyone on the street with jeans, boots, and work shirts the norm. There was one girl who did seem to stand out amongst all of them however, and as he looked around his gaze always returned to her. She was tall and thin, with a narrow face graced with shockingly blue eyes and a very thin nose. She was standing at a table, bent over towards him, at an odd angle, her thin body appearing like a broken twig partially snapped. Oddly, in those warm temperatures she wore a red wool cap with blue and yellow lines across it and strings which could be pulled down to tie underneath the chin dangling by her cheeks. He watched her as she cut vegetables with a few other workers, and his persistent gaze seemed to draw her attention, because suddenly she stopped what she was doing and stared back at him with a hard, stern stare. It made him realize he was staring, and then purposely, he looked away into any direction that was open.

Suddenly, a uniformed man appeared at the end of the compound, he carried a backpack and he wore a security man's utility belt, with equipment, and a gold name plate on his shirt which would reflect the sun as he turned about to look around the camp, as if looking for someone. Michael froze, not sure what to do, his heart racing out of his chest as he quickly searched around for a place to hide.

But when the officer turned and looked right at him, then unknowingly shifted his gaze, Michael began to breathe again as the officer obviously wasn't looking for him, but someone else.

As if on cue, Dr. Coda appeared, grasped the hand in a firm handshake, and they both smiled and seemingly at ease. Almost as quickly, a small Asian man appeared wearing the 'camp attire' yet he had on padded knee caps and wore a Cub's baseball hat backwards. He too was greeted warmly by the two men, and he was also lugging backpack. Smiling and laughing, they extended pleasantries, then the Asian gentleman gave the backpack to the officer, and the officer gave his backpack to Dr. Coda. Simultaneously they opened the sacks, and Michael almost gasped as the officer pulled out clear plastic bags of finely ground, dried leaves, and Dr. Coda in turn pulled out boxes of gauze, needles, and bandages. Satisfied, the Dr. returned everything to the bag, nodded and reached into a deep pocket on the side of his tunic. As the officer wrapped up his bundle, the Dr. gave him a small stack of papers. Taking those, the officer shoved them into his pants pocket, while they continued to exchange pleasantries.

Suddenly, the three of them stopped talking an looked directly at Michael. Awkwardly, Michael looked away as if not to notice what was in his mind a drug deal, then tried to nonchalantly spoon around he's bowl, as he tried to watch them with his peripheral vision. He saw the Asian nod, the officer squint and nod, and Dr. Coda stare stoned faced.

With the information passed, and the deal done, they all shook hands, the officer disappeared into the brush, and the Dr. lifted his bag and disappeared into one of the huts. The Asian, however, seemed intrigued by Michael, and without averting his eyes, he began to walk towards him, his gaze solid.

When the Asian reached him, Michael looked up, acted surprised, and stared back at the sullen features of the diminutive man in front of him. The Asian hesitated, smiled broadly with eyes that softened quickly, and held out a thick, earth stained hand right at Michael's chest.

"I'm Tony Wong. You'll be with me as soon as you're ready."

Michael hesitated, very leary as he tried to process what he had seen with what he was being brought into. "Okay, um…." He began, then pointed out an obvious deficiency. "I don't have any shoes."

"Oh," Toney said, slightly bewildered. "that is an issue for today. Well then, I will talk to someone and get you some shoes tomorrow morning. How do you feel otherwise?"

Michael shrugged. "Okay, just trying to see what is going on and how things work around here. By the way, what will I be doing?"

"I need help with some harvesting. An extra hand would make it go faster."

Tony shrugged. "Just seeds and dried leaves, nothing complicated, just manual work."

Testing just how far he was being pulled in, he

responded, "It can't be more than a few days as I will be leaving soon."

Unexpectedly Tony smiled broadly and reached for his hand again. "Excellent, I will see you tomorrow then." He then rose abruptly and hurriedly walked away.

Deciding not to linger much longer by the fire, he set his bowl down on the log and in a series of awkward jumps, was able to get back on his feet, making his way back to the hut from where he began. He shook his head to clear out the notice of all he had just seen and heard, and needed a refuge to sort out the facts and his options. The only place he knew where this could happen was a the hut where he was sequestered, but when he was halfway across the compound, heeding hardly any notice from the people around him, he felt a firm hand on his shoulder.

"You're doing well." A familiar voice said.

Michael turned quickly and saw his rescuer smiling broadly, dressed exactly as he was when he pulled Michael from the trailer a few days before. With the strangeness of the people he just met, this man seemed gratefully familiar and Michael felt almost glad to see him.

"Yes I am." Michael answered. Hey, listen, I never thanked you for saving me and taking care of me."

The man's face went blank and he just shrugged.

"What is your name?"

"I'm Edgar Stuffle." he replied, adjusting his glasses as if making a formal presentation.

"Thank you Edgar. Ok, "Michael began edging closer to his benefactor. "What is this place?"

"It's just a place … for people to come and just live."

"Like a commune?"

Edgar thought for a second. "No, people don't actually live here other than the Dr. and Hayden. People leave and arrive…. like you…. all the time."

"So I can leave anytime I want?"

"Sure."

"Like I can leave right now?"

"Sure but I wouldn't do that if I were you."

Michael nodded as if comprehending a veiled threat.

"You don't have any shoes, it is tough to go through the woods in socks." Edgar added.

Michael was not comprehending after all.

"How about you Edgar? Can you leave?"

"Yes, well, actually in a few weeks I will have to."

"Oh?"

"You see we can only stay a certain number of weeks, after that you have to leave."

"Or what?"

"Nothing, it's just time to leave."

"Who determines that?"

"Hayden."

There was a pause. "Why does Hayden get to decide?"

"You talk to him."

"Every day?"

"If you like."

Edgar was getting impatient now with all the questions, and was beginning to sway back and forth in is eagerness to leave.

Michael was still confused, but now at least there was an outline to work from.

"Thanks Edgar" he replied, suddenly feeling tired. "Listen, I'm going to go lay down for a while, I suddenly need some sleep."

"Ok, Catch me if you have any more questions."

"Sure." Michael replied, then turned to continue his quest towards the hut, even more uncertain of what he was now connected to and what he was now a part of. Parting the flap of the hut, he quickly laid down on his now familiar bed and quickly fell asleep.

Josef waited silently on a bench at the train station. All around him people surged and thinned as the trains arrived and departed. Since being retired, he was never in any hurry to get anywhere, so much so, that he arrived extra early for appointments so he would have time to read his book. This time was like any other; he was forty minutes early for his train and it gave him plenty of time to read a few chapters. Occasionally he would put it aside and he would watch the people. Young children reminded him of his own many years ago. Old women reminded him of his wife, young couples reminded him of Michael and Andrea and their laughter. But he didn't dwell on those thoughts he pushed out of his mind, still too much sadness and too many questions.

As his train called for boarding, he closed his book, turning of the page's corner to mark his place, then slipped into the throng of people just like him heading into the city. Rapidly moving towards the center of the car, he chose an empty three-seater. Taking a seat in the center with no one choosing to sit on either side of him, he sat quietly looking out the window collecting his thoughts, as the train rolled slowly out of the station.

Despite being in the middle of the train, he could still see out the windows as the landscape began to change from green landscapes of tree lined boulevards and parks, to one of tall buildings and concrete facades. Factories began to replace schools and apartment buildings began to replace homes, the rail lie itself began to get wider as more tracks merged and ran parallel. Children would squeal at eh sudden rush of a train passing in the opposite direction, then laugh at their own silliness. After four stops, they were in the city, close to the center, and they were now in the canyon of office buildings and towers.

His destination was only a few more stops, on the other side of the down town, and he began to move restlessly in anticipation. Every month or so he would make this journey. He looked forward to it, yet grew anxious as the day grew closer. It was his journey back to his old neighborhood where he had lived for forty-five years, raised his family and buried his wife. He knew the anxiety wasn't about the visit, his friends were waiting for him at the usual place, it was the changes he saw when he stepped off the train. The businesses that had closed, and the new ones starting up, selling odd products he could never understand that people needed.

Finally passing through the downtown, the steel and glass towers fading away again to brick and mortar buildings, he gripped his book tightly and pulled himself out of his seat, proceeding down the aisle to the doors. Reaching the doors just as they opened, he stepped off with only a few people joining him and stood on the platform, trying to stay out of the way of the commuters getting on.

The station was of the old architecture, having been built when trains were the only transportation to get anywhere far. Around him he could see the yellow brick apartments, some with the art deco facades of the thirties, others in red brick with limestone corners. This was home, and as he followed the stairs down to the street from the platform, he passed through a revolving door that put him in the center of a robust neighborhood. The smells now came back to him, the bitter fumes of diesel from the buses, the sounds of rustling people around him and the sharp wind as a flurry of cars sped past in a hurry to stop. Nearby a vendor held up the morning edition of the paper, his calls of 'Paper' having been worn down to only 'PA...PA...PA'. Renewed from the vibrancy and energy around him, he turned and walked up the block, past a dirty sleeping man in the corner, his legs halfway across the sidewalk, to underneath the railroad trestle where a giant freight engine idled it's turbine, and other to a small stand where a small man sold....everything. Josef approached the store and passed through the narrow door and into a collection of gum, postcards, chips, and magazines. On the sides were small coolers with drinks and freezers with ice cream.

Reaching for a weekly magazine, he laid it on the varnished wooden counter, and reached for his wallet. As if on cue, a young man with a piercing through the center of his nose rose up, examined the magazine and the man, then turned a mobild scanner towards Josef. For a second they gazed at each other.

"Just scan your card and it's done." The young man said.

"What card?" Josef asked.

"Whatever you want to pay with?"

"How about cash?' Josef said and pulled out a $20 bill.

The young man shrugged. "That works."

Having bought the magazine and received his change, Josef stared at him for a few seconds and asked with brutal honestly.

"Doesn't that hurt?'

The young man looked at him with a furrowed brow, then pointed at his piercing.

"You mean this?"

"Ya, that."

Nodding his head in thought, "When it gets cold I take it out. Bu then I get a new one in the spring." He then smiled at Josef and threw it back to him. "You should get one."

Josef smiled in return, "I did, only I call it shrapnel." Rolling up the magazine, he tapped the young man on the shoulder. "Tell your grandfather I said I hope he gets better."

"Sure Joe."

With that, he turned and walked out of the store, heading for his final destination, only a few blocks away.

As he walked out of the convenience store, he felt a

strength in his step. His familiarity was back and with it came a powerful energy. These were his streets and his buildings, and his neighbors, although he wasn't unaware of the younger faces replacing the older ones. Every so often, he recollects and thinks that perhaps Andrea was right, it was time to move away. Prune out the dead so to speak and let the new growth blossom. But on a day like today, the smells and sounds all around him thickened is blood, sharpened is mind, and made him think that just for today, this was his neighborhood again.

Walking the two blocks to a small windowless corner bar, Josef pushed open the solid, heavy red metal door, and stepped into a small tavern with a long bar on the side with a long mirror in the back of it which reflected the entire room making it appear that it had twice the space it didn't have. The low light shadowed the chairs and tables, but the reflection of the liquor bottles in the mirror; their amber and blue hues, made it seen as if they were gems in a mine.

For a few seconds, he hesitated, his eighty year old pupils expanded to gulp in as much light as possible, but he knew the terrain by heart. He hadn't taken two steps when he was slapped on the back by a burly pipefitter heading out into the afternoon sun.

"Glad to see ya Joe!!!" he bellowed, but was out of earshot when Josef replied "Hi ya Samuel!"

Greetings sprouted like sirens as he made his way along the bar and to a large table in the back filling up a small open room adjacent to the main bar.

"Hey Joe!"

"Look at the stranger from the suburbs."

"Hi Joe."

"What ya having today Joe?" the bartender asked, a generation younger than Josef, so just passed retirement age.

"What's new?" Josef replied.

"Got the first keg of the Oktoberfest brew in."

Josef gave him a thumb's up, and in the same motion, reached for the freshly tapped beer on the bar.

Taking just the slightest sip, he half shuffled his way to a waiting chair across from the four men already seated equidistant round the table.

As he approached, he raised his free hand in acknowledgement as he licked the foam from his upper lip. "Josef!" the cry rose in a low murmur as he was recognized throughout the group. The man closest to him patted the seat of the open remaining chair. "Have a seat!" a tall man with thin black hair exclaimed. His face was narrow, his eyes dark and direct, but his smile was easy, showing off a clean set of false teeth perfectly formed, like Stonehenge itself.

This was Rudolf, Josef's best and longest running friend.

"Hello my knights!" Josef exclaimed as he placed his glass down and sat roughly into the designated chair.

This was the roundtable, composed of men that spent their lives building. Rudolf started out as a machinist like Josef. They met on the first job Josef ever had, rarely spent a day apart until he moved.

Seated next to him was Klaus the electrician, small

of stature, but stout with thick fingers from years of bending conduit and wire. Next to him was Willy, the steel worker. He was always wore sunglasses, his eyes fading from years around the spark s of forged iron. The last was Erst. He wasn't in the factories like the other men, he sold insurance, but he blended in with them through the [paths emerging from the past. All were from a wasted Germany, all wer young men at the time with their own tragedies and journeys until they wound up here in this neighborhood tied together forever through heritage and tragedy.

As soon as Josef sat down the stories began and the old men began to shed their age and for a few hours they were young lions again, trading stores of success and failure, desire and experiences. Stores that were told over and over again, becoming more ingrained and richer as they were revived.

In a midst of a story told by Ernst of two nurses and how he made them late for work the next day, Rudolf turned to Josef.

"Sorry to hear about the boy." He said solemnly.

Josef shrugged. "It's a mystery."

"How's Andrea doing?"

"She's ok, but it's the not knowing that is eating her up."

Rudolf just nodded, reflecting on all the people he knew as a young man and how they vanished, forever, him never knowing their fate. "I understand," he said, "then looked into Josef's face. "You understand."

Josef nodded.

"Hey, listen," Rudolf began changing the subject and placing his hand on Josef's forearm. "How is the new place?"

Josef shrugged "I've lived in worst places."

"Seriously?"

"It's okay, Josef conceded. "I'm close to the girl. It works."

"Guess what I'm doing." Rudolf said, leaning back and crossing his arms.

"What?"

"I'm going back."

"To Germany?"

Rudolf nodded.

"for how long?" Josef asked.

"Till it's over." And he clenched a fist by his heart, suddenly flaying his fingers out like an explosion.

"Really." Josef asked.

"Really." Rudolf followed up. "it's time." He said. "my sister is there…in Cologne… I can stay with her until I find my own place."

"It's different." Josef said.

"It is … and it isn't"

He smiled at Josef with a grin of absolute completion. "It's home. My time here is done."

Josef thought deeply and nodded, oblivious of the chatter around him, yet very aware of the change about to befall him. He reached into his pocket he touched the bent spoon.

Detective Bateman clicked his phone off concerned about the conversation he just had and slowly walked back down the hallway towards the apartment. Despite the dull yellow paint and the threadbare carpet, the air was brittle with chlorine, a sign that it may not be clean, but it is sanitized. Along the walls were long thin scratches like racing stripes, left by hundreds of dressers, entertainment centers, and bookshelves carted back and forth as occupants left and new ones arrived.

Walking into the room, he almost collided with an evidence technician as he was walking out. When dealing with an event like the explosion, everything is investigated to be sure terrorism wasn't an option, As such, investigating the apartment of a transient male that was obliterated in an explosion at a populated site takes all of the depts. efforts.

"We'll be out in about thirty minutes." The lieutenant leading the investigation bellowed from across the living room. Bateman nodded, placed his hands on his hips and scanned the sparse room. Little furniture, errant piles of dirty clothes, ancient leftover takeout food in the refrigerator, and a laptop on the floor with scattered papers and bills all around it. The complete disarray and lack of focus was the trademark of a single man with little responsibility and no desire for accountability. The clinching factor for the occupant's harmlessness was the catalog porn discs on the upper shelf of a closet with only 5 shirts and two pairs of pants; kept in a pristine folder and organized alphabetically.

Stepping carefully over the male detritus scattered around the cheap carpet, he glanced quickly at the areas tagged, surfaces dusted, and photographs staged. He knew already what the report would say – no link to terrorism or other predetermining factors attributing to an terrorist act. Case closed.

Just to get some air away from a stifling room full of the city's finest, he opened the patio door and walked about onto a thin concrete slab of a balcony with a rusting white railing around it. Barely enough room to turn around, he reached down and moved the metal folding chair with a bent leg, knocking over five empty beer cans like bowling pins. Uncomfortable with the awkwardness, he took in the soft wind as his tie fishtailed around his neck, closing his eyes and breathing in the gentle breeze and he actually felt the weight of the case physically lift his brain.

After inhaling deeply a few times, he opened his eyes and looked over the forest preserve which stretched endlessly before him, a nice canopy of billowing green trees seemingly within stepping distance of the patio. How nice, he thought, it would be to just shed everything like an old skin and walk away deep into the forests, far, far away from everything. Bringing everything to its simplest form. Turning facts from esoteric to actual. To escape and only focus on the fundamentals, Emerson at his finest.

His attention as suddenly pulled back by the vibrating phone on his hip. Gone quickly were the towering trees and endless plains. Now it was back to someone missing. Snatching it off his belt, he hesitated for a second, then pushed to answer, sliding the phone next to his ear, and bending his head in concentration.

"Detective Bateman." He mumbled.

"Have you found anything?" Andrea's voice chirped over the earpiece; calm, but direct.

:Just the final pieces to the victims' lifestyle, nothing out of the ordinary." He stated, trying to be official, but leaving some reassurance that nothing was deliberate.

There was a hesitation on her part. "Would you tell me?" Equally hesitant, he offered honestly "Yes." Quickly he followed up. "How are you doing?"

Surprised at the personal response, she replied. "Ok." Feeling guilty and just a quick response she added. "The kids are doing well also, surprisingly good. They had a lot questions at first, but now they seem pretty sure that I'm not going anywhere and they are back in their routines.

"Good." He replied confidently, "But you haven't answered the question. How are you doing?

Silence. "Still hurts. I mean he could be dead, just not there, or he could have lost his wallet and someone had picked it up and they had it with them at the restaurant." She stopped. "I think of a lot of things."

"I understand." He ended abruptly, creating an awkward silence in hopes of trapping some information. "Listen." He added "if I brought over some Chinese food later, would you be interested?"

"Sure." She replied quickly. "Well, the kids really don't like it."

"It's not for them."

"Ok." Was the soft reply.

"After 7?" he added.

"Ok, I guess that's fine."

"See you then." And he quickly signed off to get the text coming through

Seeing it, he cradled the phone in his hands and read the single ling. Typing: 'Working on it. More information soon.' He hesitated, then pushed send, snapped the phone back on his hip, and rising from the chair strode back into the apartment.

CHAPTER IV

Edgar stumbled into the hut, his face flushed with anxiety and his eyes wild with fear. He shuffled over to the center, where Hayden was sitting crossed legged quietly on a nest of pillows, a thick book open midway, it's dark brown pages giving away it's age.

Reaching Hayden, Edgar flopped down in front, falling sideways, his short arms propping up his torso while his legs lay useless next to him. Hayden stared at him intently, the silence punctuated only by Edgar's rapid shallow breathing.

"I had the dream again." He blurted out, wiping a stream of sweat off his neck.

Hayden nodded. Then reached down next to his leg and softly picked up a long necked butane lighter. Reaching over to his left, he grasped a large candle in a shallow open mouthed jar. He did this four times until there were four candles equidistant in front of him.

"Do you want to tell me?" Hayden said quietly.

Edgar contemplated the decision, one that he seemed to be reflecting even as he entered the hut. He looked at the candles, and then pulled his legs up so he was on his knees, sitting on his heels.

"Yes, he said.

Hayden put the lighter back and laced his fingers over the book, leaning forward lightly with his shoulders, his eyes bright, but sharp, brow furrowed with attention.

Edgar took another deep breath, which seemed to set him right and bring his confidence up.

"I'm in the attic of the house," he jumbled out for clarity. "and I'm going through boxes and I find the chest, and it is big and blue with a heavy metal clasp." He held out his palm upright to give a sense of dimension. His eyes began to drift now, as if describing a picture over Hayden' shoulder.

"So I open it and I see her dress. Her favorite one, the one that she would cook in. I held it up by the shoulders and looked at it, then folded it and placed it back into the chest. I then turned away to open another box and I felt his warmth on my shoulders and also a tightening and I turned to look and …… his eyes widened now and he began to breathe quicker, as he relived it. "… it was her, she was there."

He paused. "So I stood up and reached out and pulled her close. It was so close I could feel her breathing and I could feel the tightness of her arms as she hugged me."

Edgar's eyes dropped to the floor, his shoulders slumped, and he crossed his arms over his chest as he relived it. "But then as I held tighter, she began to fade. Like sand draining out of a bag, and as I squeezed tighter, it faded faster until I was holding this empty dress."

He then held out his arms, palms up helpless. "Then the dress crumpled and fell to the floor and laid there like a pile of ashes."

Hayden listened intently, then nodded solemnly.

Edgar stood and walked over to a narrow shelf by the door. Over it was a small curtain which hid the contents, and when he parted it, he removed a long string of beads. On it were small beads of red, yellow, green and blue. Returning to Hayden, he resumed his seat and held the necklace out over his fingers. "I'm sad today." He replied, as Hayden blew out one of the candles.

Peter parked his car close to the yellow tape fluttering in the breeze. That enclosed the burned out restaurant. As a barrier it had served its purpose and kept the curious out and the evidence in, but it had been two weeks since the explosion, and the elements had begun to work their effects. The tape had snapped and flapped itself effortlessly whenever a breeze came up. The rains had soaked the blackened ruins. The glaze of water shimmered over the hardened smoke stained furniture and the puddling in the low patches of the asphalt seemed like mirrors. Glass was still strewn over every surface, glistening in the sunlight, like seashells on the beach. Blood stains had blended into the sidewalk around the building, darkening the light grey stone in irregular blotches.

Scanning the scene again, he pulled out his badge, hung it from his neck on a chain – and nodded to the day officer seated in the cruiser not far away. He glanced at the small piles of sentimental offerings doting the light poles and debris on the extreme edges of the lot. Like pagan offerings for a good harvest, or Indian tributes for a good hunt, these memorials dotted the scene. But as the elements took their toll, the bright pink teddy bears and ribboned bouquets bad faded away to the dulled colors of gray and brown. Thousands had been trucked away, but they kept coming until the refuse men gave up and let them pile up. Now that the bulldozers were parked in the lot next door, it was their task to eliminate the remainder when they took the building down.

Crossing his arms in front of the shell of the restaurant, he tried for the hundredth time to visualize where Michael was and where he could be. If he was in the restaurant, how did he survive? Surely he was unharmed and walked away. His car was here, unless he knew someone that could drive him away. But if someone had met him, how could they predict the explosion? Walking around, he stepped on the crushed glass and shredded material, struggling at times to walk.

For convenience, he found a clear spot in front of the ATM machine. Regaining his balance, he stood and glanced at his new perspective. Initially it seemed the same junk; different view. From his vantage point, he could clearly see the parking lot, the seating, and some of the counter. He turned and looked at the ATM machine and concrete pillar which seemed to close off the end of the counter. He shook his head slowly as he marveled at the glowing screen of the bank machine, still functional and willing after being in the center of a tempest. "These things are built like tanks." He said aloud, then he hesitated as a fact suddenly registered in his head.

Looking up, then down, then around, he saw the blast marks all around him, except for in the front of the machine. "This is actually more like a bunker." He said again, then looked down at the floor where he was standing. He saw blackened wisps of scorch wrapping around the machine, where the ballast had pushed out from the counter, around the pillar, and dovetailed back together to complete the wave of destruction. Moving his feet to get a better sense of the direction, he saw a small piece of evidence that wouldn't have mattered to anyone other than him; a bloody shoe print.

Following a hunch, he took out his smart phone, moving the screen to get as full a picture as possible, then snapped it. Taking a few more to get the best picture, he also took off his own shoe to get a n estimated size. Finishing his thought, he remembered crisp $20 bills in Michael's billfold, and a bankcard that matched the establishment that owned the ATM. Using his phone one more time, he speed dialed Adrienne, shuffling impatiently as it rang. Disappointed at the voice mail, he quickly collected his thoughts and waited for the tone. Getting only voice mail he replied; "Yes Andrea, this is Detective Batemen. Just a quick question – could you check your bank accounts and see if there was a withdrawal at the location of the restaurant. Let me know as soon as possible, thanks."

Clicking it off, he retraced everything he learned, then tried to complete his thoughts and hoped he had some luck at finishing his conclusion Flipping through the photo gallery, he selected the best photo he could, displayed it on his screen, then looked away at the debris around him with a totally different perspective.

Selecting a possible path, and the assumed direction of a man who didn't want to be found, he could only make a guess on what he would do, then walked off the premises towards a collection of semi trailers in the distance. Reaching the end of the debris field, he then began a coordinated grid search, using his experience and a map in his head.

Quickly he discovered a bloody shoe, print, then another of the same print about two feet away, then another, then another, all leading towards the trailers. Holding his phone down, he replicated the same procedure as the footprint by the ATM, even comparing the shoe size again.

Having gathered the evidence, he then walked towards the trailers, cautiously studying the tracks to follow where they lead looking for any deviation. He registered that the strides were getting closer, possibly from the pain, until he reached the trailers, Scanning under the nearest trailer he saw the pool of dried blood, and then something unusual. A thin line of blood leading away from it, one more footprint by the end of the trailer, then nothing, as he just evaporated into thin air. Taking more pictures, he played out scenarios in his mind as he looked all around the trailer, the adjacent parking lot, and the thick wall of foliage bordering the forest preserve.

Josef walked into the library, a steno notebook clenched tightly in his left hand, his walked strong and determined as he strode through the revolving door and past the reception desk and then the large glaring poster on the metal stand welcoming all to the library and to visit the new children's wing. He had slept little the night before in anticipation of this, and the anticipation now fueled his desire to accomplish what he wanted to do.

Having spent many hours here, he knew the layout as well as his own house. Reaching the elevator, he took it to the third floor, where he disembarked, went down two hallways, and reached the 'Computer Lab' He was lucky, there was no one there and he quickly slid behind an open screen, only glancing at the sign warning of a 30 minute limit.

Cautiously, he opened the screen with his password, searched for a geography site, then licked on the title page to enter the domain. Immediately the site displayed a colorful view from space of a slowly spinning earth, with the prompt box asking the question "Where would you like to go?"

Setting the notebook down on the desk next to the mouse pad, he flipped up the cover and studied the dozen or so lines of numbers and street names. All night he had written down all the addresses and numbers that he could remember. Even if he thought that his how it was spelled, he wrote it down, if nothing else, but to trigger another memory.

Deliberately he tapped out the address, up to the city and country. Hesitating, he then double checked it with what he had written, then taped the mouse to allow the function. Suddenly the screen zoomed over to Europe, then centered on Germany, then to his city, then to a line of roofs in a grid pattern, where it stopped with no indication of where he was. Perplexed, he leaned back in his chair, searching the screen for some direction.

"Can I help you?' a young woman in a bright sweater asked as she leaned over the desk.

"Yes, I am trying to find this address and it seems that the machine doesn't understand."

"Ok, let me see." She said as she deftly moved about the screen and in second had the answer.

"I'm sorry that address doesn't exist. Are you sure you have it spelled correctly?"

"Yes, Here …here is another address, try this one."

She typed in the address, again the screen held steady, not revealing any secrets.

The two sat there for a few moments, him perplexed by the science, her working for a solution around the problem.

"Is there a landmark that you can use?' she asked, pushing her long black hair back over her ear, and with the same motion adjusted her glasses.

"Yes!" Josef blurted out, then typed in the name of the one landmark he had hoped would still be there. Finishing, he hit enter, and waited for a few moments. Slowly the screen shifted to another part of the city, centering on a large open market square. He could now clearly see the center of the plaza, and the large circular forms in the center.

"Does that look familiar?" she asked.

"Yes." he replied hesitantly.

"Here, let's do this." She said smiling now confident that they had the answers. With a click and drag, the screen suddenly magnified, then in a flash, he was looking a the plaza as if in a movie, the center fountain clearly visible in front of him, just as he had seen it decades before as a boy.

"That's it." He said incredulous.

"Ok, now using these arrows, you can go forward or backward, or down any street that you would like."

As amazing as the technology was, even more incredulous was the pictures of a modern city, resuscitated and improved. In still life, he could see citizens young and old frozen in time, living in an area he left as desolated. Cautiously moving the arrows, he scanned over the buildings and the streets, then turned a corner and ventured down a street rebuilt and renewed.

Gaining confidence, he ventured back, then proceeded down another, then before him, a survivor as much a witness as himself, stood in front of him. The stone cathedral shadowed over the street as it had over the charred ruins decades before. The gargoyles still grinned and cackled at the parishioners as they had for centuries, almost as if they had grown stronger from the hell around them that day, gaining energy from the carnage all around them.

"Is this what you were looking for?' she asked, now standing over him arms crossed with the confidence of someone who had given the keys of a new world to a small child. His silence was the answer. Seeing him studying the cathedral, she offered one more nugget of information. "Can I show you something?"

He looked up in wonder at her, still in awe by what he was staring at. She bent over one last time, moved the mouse around, then clicked an icon at the top of the screen. Suddenly, with a slow hum, the small box printer next to him began to work, sliding a sheet of paper with a photograph of the cathedral squarely in front of him. Taking it and holding it in front of him, she completed her instruction. "If you need any more help, let me know I'll be glad to assist."

Josef just nodded as the catalog of photos he wanted to take began to fill his mind, he began to move the mouse around in his journey into a new vision of the past.

Michael stumbled out of the hut, and looked around the complex blurry eyed, trying to get his bearings, He stretched his legs now and for the first time, felt one hundred percent; no pain, no tightness, just the awkwardness of sleep.

In passing, Dr. Coda noticed him and reached out to him. "Perfect timing." He said joyfully. "come with me, the Mule is here."

Obediently, Michael fell in behind him, still rubbing his eyes. When he had regained his sight, Michael realized that he was at the center council fire, looking at a tall man with layers upon layers of shoes stung over his shoulders. They were of all types and sizes. 'Work boots, sandals, snow boots, moccasins, tennis shoes, even flip-flops. Pairs were tied together, then collected into bunches and slung over his shoulders as so much baggage. Some were new, others worn and scuffed, but the sheer volume of footwear extended beyond his frame a few feet, giving him a barrel shape, like the clown in the vaudeville show.

With an unusually gleeful sense of anticipation, the Dr. presented the supplier to Michael. "Tell him your shoe size."

Michael looked the creature up and down cautiously, then replied "10 ½"

Thinking for a second, the man brokered a huge smile, peeled two strands of shoes off his left shoulder, to reach a third, which he pulled away and gave to Michael. There was a collection of twelve pairs of shoes, six on each end in a diverse variety of types. Looking them over, he was leaning towards a casual brown Rockport, then the Dr. interjected.

"Choose the heavier tennis shoe. You will be more comfortable in the coming weeks."

Selecting just such a pair in a dark green he slipped them on and tied them up,. Comfortable, he nodded and shrugged his shoulders.

"Excellent." The Dr. said. Turning to the Mule, he shook his hand gratefully as the man began to reassemble his load.

"I'm supposed to help in the field today?" Michael asked.

"Actually, there has been a change. You're not needed there today, You are going with Edgar into the city."

Michael hesitated. "I'm not sure that is smart. I really think I should stay here."

"Won't be a problem. You will be in areas that I'm sure you don't know. No one will know you…. If you are comfortable with that?"

"Sure." He said.

As if on cue, Edgar shuffled over after leaving the leader's hut and stood sheepishly to one side, waiting for the conversation to end.

"Edgar." The doctor began, turning towards him. Take this gentleman with you. Make sure you have everything you need."

Nodding, Edgar motioned Michael to follow him. "What you need is in the satchels by the sign post. Be sure to follow the regular route." The doctor added as they followed a path to the edge of the compound.

Reaching the edge of the compound, there was a tall post, unnamed despite its distinction, where there were four stuffed recyclable bags positioned neatly at its base. Edgar motioned for Michaels to grab two, while he took up the other two. Despite their heft they were surprisingly light. Looking into the second one, he saw bundled packages in brown paper, neatly stacked. Without any acknowledgment, Edgar proceeded up a thin bare trail leading towards a small part in the foliage. IN a second, he was wrapped with the cool of the forest and the thin darkness of the unknown.

They followed the trail through the woods for about 30 minutes, until it came out next to a busy highway, and the post of a bus stop. The sound of the traffic made him uneasy in addition to the anonymity he was trying to preserve. The bus appeared quickly and with Edgar presenting a pass, pulled from deep in his breast pocket, they boarded the bus with a half dozen distracted people on it. Sitting close to the back, three rows away from anyone, they situated the bags between their legs, and with Michael situated next to the window, Edgar leaned towards him to give his instructions.

"When we get off the bus, follow me close, I will be walking fast; with purpose. When you walk like you have a destination, people ignore you. When you wander looking around, you draw attention, particularly from the police. Also, you don't talk, I talk. If you need to talk to someone, talk to me. Got it?"

Michael nodded, Edgar smiled.

As they sat on the bus, his confidence began to build as his anxiety recessed. Being on public transportation, everyone followed the rules and kept to themselves; immersed in I-phone screens, flipping pages in magazines, or in most cases staring aimlessly out the window, watching the time pass, deep in thought.

"How long have you been in the community?" Michael asked softly, hoping not to rupture his companion's serious concentration.

"About 10 weeks." He replied.

"So you are almost out?"

"Sort of, because I was able to contribute a new member, I get an extra week, so now I have 3 weeks to go. But I can leave whenever I want to." He quickly added.

"What's your story?" Michael asked.

Edgar thought for a second. "Not much of a story." He looked down into his lap, his fingers laced tightly, one thumb over the other. "My mom died. Not much to tell there. Everyone dies."

"Was it expected?"

"She was old, I lived with her my whole life, and she was always there. She had like a cold or the flu, and one morning I woke up and went to check on her…. And it was over."

"So how did you end up here?"

"After the funeral, I just sat in the living room, I think for a few days because I remember waking up on the couch a few times and I remember being hungry."

"Were you by yourself?"

"Yea. I don't have any real family. My dad left when I was a little kid never saw him again. No brothers or sisters." he squinted trying to pull facts from the deep recesses of his memory. "Some cousins but I haven't seen them in years. Don't even remember what they look like."

He took a deep breath,. "Anyway, I just realized that for some reason I couldn't stay there anymore, so I packed up a few clothes in a small bag that I could carry, and left. Just started walking."

"Did you just walk through the woods and find the place?"

"No, Dr. Coda found me. I was getting some food behind a grocery store, when he appeared with the bags we have now. He promised me that if I helped him, he would give me a safe place to go. He was lucky in a way, he wasn't very strong an I suppled the muscle to carry his load.

"Is it a safe place like he said?"

"Yes, very safe." Abruptly ending the conversation, Edgar looked out the window, reached up and pulled the 'STOP' cord, and began to gather his bundle.

"Get ready to go, our stop is next."

Without further comment, Michael picked up his load, shuffled across the vacant seat Edgar had just left, and stepped into the aisle behind his guide.

The bus ride had been another half hour, the sparse suburban landscape with wide streets and low buildings was now replaced by the density of a developed population. Having reached a section of the city he was unfamiliar with, Edgar led as they disembarked and walked two more blocks to their first destination.

In the center of the block they were walking towards a large grocery store. Not a typical one that he was used to, but a specialized one that provided fresh fish, chicken, and wholesome, natural foods.

Walking past it, they went around the end of the block and approached from the alley in back. There were three brown steel doors there, each marked with a different letter. Going to the middle one marked 'D' Edgar placed his two satchels down, then banged loudly on the door. The noise seemed surprisingly muffled, and they had to wait for a few minutes before it swung open, a small thin man with a shaved head and thick black glasses stood in the doorway, glaring at both of them.

He nodded at Edgar, a motion of acknowledgement, then reached out and took his two bags. Propping the doorway open with one foot, he reached inside, and presented Edgar with two identical bags, only instead of brown packages, they were bursting with fruits and vegetables. Michael even thought he saw some sausages showing out of the top before they settled towards the bottom of the bag.

"How's the Dr?" the man asked quickly.

Edgar shrugged. "The same."

"Give him my best." The man said before disappearing back into the store, the door behind him slamming firmly shut with a solid thud.

"Let's go." Edgar said shouldering the new burden with ease.

"Where to?" Michael asked.

"Next stop of course." Edgar added as he began to move down the alley." Remember, walk like you're going somewhere and no one will bother you."

"But we are going somewhere." Michael bleated.

"Don't argue, just keep up."

Sitting in his usual booth, the Boss, blared at his I phone, the screen reflecting in the half finished glass of whisky next to him. He was working which is why he waved the waitress off twice, and watched undisturbed as his 'Number One' slipped into the seat across from him. "What's the line on the game tonight?" he asked in a low voice.

"Fourteen, home team." Was the reply, "but the other outlets are calling it a trap game."

The boss chuckled softly. "Superstition can be very profitable. Looking up wondrously at the ceiling, he added. "The final refuge of the ignorant." He said in a grandiose manner.

"I have other news. That guy you told me to keep looking for, he's not dead. Turns out he survived the blast and wandered off somewhere. Now, everyone is looking for him."

"Any information 'everyone' doesn't have?"

"Our source is still gathering facts. As soon as he gets a hit, he will let you know." The man leaned forward slightly, "He will call you directly."

The boss nodded and looked back as his screen while the waitress brought the Number One his usual brandy. She lingered, as the boss set down his phone, swallowed the last of his glass, the ice crackling in anticipation and then finally nodded at her for another.

"Keep looking for him. Even if we don't get our money, he needs to be the example for the others." Quickly receiving his drink from her, he rose unexpectedly, sliding the cell phone into his breast pocket, fisting his glass and walked towards the front of the bar.

Being early afternoon, the crowd was very thin, only the regulars and a few students were there, so there was no intimidation in a casual walk through the aisle, With his assistant walking close behind, he strode to the large plate glass window facing the street at the front of the bar, revealing a vibrant yet antiquated neighborhood.

Standing in front of the window like a lord overlooking the county from his castle, he took a long sip, smacking his lips loudly when he was finished.

"In fact, I think I will take care of this one myself. I

could use the workout." A broad grin engulfed his face, distracted by the complete sense of power, oblivious to the two roughshod men walking passed him carrying bags and driven by a determined pace of purpose.

Peter waited on the park bench and watched the children in the playground fumbling and tossing themselves over the plastic and rubber obstacles, designed to build minds and bodies. He slung his arm over the back casually and crossed his legs in solace. He tried to do this openly because it was a relaxing afternoon, and by stretching his arms out, his coat opened and revealed his badge. It lowered the anxiety of the parents, knowing that he was a cop and not some sick bastard after their kids.

In the years since he had been coming here, he had seen a change in the population. More kids of different colors, more languages, more patience, and a lot more dads. How different this was from his childhood, where his father was rarely seen and the one thing he would do, required a suit and tie. From him to get on the floor and play with him was unheard of, now he watched as fathers became super heroes and robots and dinosaurs for their kids.

He was smiling at a young boy in bib overalls trying tie manipulate a series of spinning blocks, when he felt a warm hand on his knuckles. Turning, he saw his father turning around the bench, his arms open.

Peter rose grasped his father tightly, his dad returning the hug with a firm grip and a pat on the back.

"How are you dad?" Peter said softly.

"Strong." His father replied. "Getting stronger every day. The pain from the arthritis is ….less, much less."

Peter smiled. "It's been awhile. What are you up to?"

"Remember when I told you I was moving back to Germany?" Rudolph said with a mischievous twinkle in his eye. I've booked it. Three months from now I'm on my way."

Peter grinned. "Good Dad, very good. And the business?"

Rudolph shrugged, his well-fitting suit moving fluidly. "Time to go."

"Surprised you made it this long. Thought it would have killed you long ago."

Rudolph thought for a second. "Luck, and connections. Like all businesses."

"Are you giving it all to Ernie, or splitting it up?'

"He'll get it all. He's ready. Unless….." Rudolph turned his head and held out an open hand, palm up.

Peter laughed. "I was at the fork in the road a long time ago. I've chosen this road." He looked over the city playground and the skyscrapers around the edge; Mountains before the valley.

"You sure? No wife, no kids, Are you happy?"

"Yes." He answered quickly. "Being a cop ….it's not just a life – it's a lifestyle." He turned and looked at his dad. "No regrets."

"You'll have regrets." Rudolph began. "I remember…."

Peter cut him off by retrieving his arm, uncrossing his leg and straightening his coat. "I know dad, I know. But you're regrets aren't my problem. I have made my choices and I will live with them. I love what I do. I couldn't be happy doing anything else. When Ernie and I were kids, you chose not to be around. Not to have any part in what we were doing."

"It was a different time." Was Rudolph's defense.

"You chose your occupation. I have chosen mine. Don't dump your guilt on me. That's not fair." Peter said directly, no emotion, just facts.

"I wish I could make you understand."

"You can't ….." You've tried and you can't." Peter exhaled sharply. "Let's start a different conversation." Peter turned and faced is father. Even at his advanced age, he still presented a formidable force he didn't like to give up on a point in a conversation, but he knew his son. This tact would only lead to an argument, and that was not how he wanted to spend the day.

Rudolf laced his fingers, and placed them harmlessly in his lap. "So how's work?" asked very simply smiling politely. "Have you any leads with this missing person?"

Back in familiar territory, Peter understood the effort he was trying to make. "Not yet." Peter answered, realizing the topic had been switched to his favorite topic – work. "but we are gathering some interesting clues…."

Michael adjusted quickly to Edgar's fast pace, and in realizing the wisdom of the street, he noticed that they were seldom given a second look or even an interesting glance. After walking about 15 blocks, they now came to a brick and limestone monstrosity filing the corner of the full city block. Pausing on the corner, Michael looked up at the twenty stories of elaborate art-deco and gilded cornices. The front door was graced with an elegant black and gold canopy; the lettering rounded in a cursive script spelled out '**Manchester Arms**' across the street side and over the sidewalk. Michael was familiar with this place. His grandmother lived here for some time, the red plush chairs, ornate lamps and oil paintings giving the effect that this was no ordinary retirement home. This was a museum where people entombed themselves. A mausoleum of living beings supported by their successful monetary efforts in life and the insufferable air surrounding them that only a few like them can truly inhale.

With his direction set, Edgar turned down the block with Michael in tow. Turning into a narrow alley leading to the back of the building, the two of them walked passed neatly arranged and rust free dumpsters, power washed concrete glistened, and the used detritus of discard was absent. It was as clear as his driveway back home. Walking around a containerized dumpster as big as a semi, they came up to another grey steel door.

This time Edgar didn't knock, he just waited patiently, until it burst open with a thrust of a neatly dressed and trimmed man in a white uniform. He propped the door open with his foot, reaching within the doorway to retrieve two carryall sacks. Seamlessly they swapped the two remaining bags with brought with these two new ones. Within a few seconds the exchange was complete. Once again they were on the move.

With the exchanges complete, Michael assumed they were on their way back to the encampment, but

Edgar had one more stop in mind. It wasn't far away and very quickly they were walking up the broad stairs and entering the towering cathedral of St. Ives Catholic church, its bell ringing has it had for over a hundred years, calling parishioners to afternoon mass.

As they entered through the thick oaken door, Michael became more curious and slightly in awe of the pageantry. The softened hymens of the organ created a gentle atmosphere as he and Edgar chose a pew near the rear of the church, some distance from the small crowd gathered at the front.

"Why are we here?" Michael asked as the ceremony began and they selected the center of the pew to sit.

But Edgar was in his own zone and looked around feverishly, before settling in for the start of the ceremony.

Edgar leaned over to Michael and raised the index finger on his left hand to accentuate his point. "Listen very carefully to what he says."

They sat quietly through the hymns and dedications, the readings and the invocation. Michael became more interested in the colorful grace of the images in the stained glass windows, the architecture of the vaulted rood and the engineering of how could they possibly change the light bulbs from a chandelier all the way up there?

Michael suddenly jerked to attention (having begun to nod off) when Edgar nudged him, sat up ramrod straight, and reached underneath his jacket to pull out a small collection of cardboard pieces, all of them about 12" x 18" in dimension.

Trying to ascertain why he would do this, Michael

looked around and noticed that the priest was walking up to the lectern. He now had that deep ache in the pit of his stomach that something was not going to go well.

"Praise be to God." The priest began. Then hesitated as he collected his thoughts. He appeared as a worldly man, late in years with thick grey hair. A man that seemed to have experienced life's extremes, yet, was refined by the experiences, not worn down.

"In all of our lives, there is one constant, and that constant is change. From the change of the seasons, to the change of the weather, to the change in or own destinies, change is all around us. And among this change, comes anxiety and fear and sometimes anger as we try to grasp what will happen. 'What will become of us tomorrow?' We ask ourselves."

He pauses, raises his right hand as if holding back the questions from the audience, "But there is one constant. The love and faith in our belief in God and his wisdom in presenting us with only that which will make us stronger."

Like a rocket, Edgar shot up his arms with his homemade sign visible only to the priest. Michael leaned forward to see what it said, and gasped as the words "YOUR'RE LYING." Showing out in thick red letters. Looking around, Michael grasped Edgar's arm in an attempt to pull it down. "Stop doing that!!" Michael said hoarsely, "They'll kick us out and we will get arrested."

"Not possible."

Edgar replied severely 'This is a church and the people's house. I'm one of the people and I can say anything I want."

Unfazed by the single's man rebellion, the priest continued, un-swayed in this thoughts and organized in his presentation and his message. Undaunted, he proceeded with the rapt attention of the audience looking at him and, not the anarchist behind them.

"...from God's love, we can draw strength and fortitude and purpose. From our belief in Him, we can be assured that however our challenges end, we can be certain it is with God's will."

Edgar dropped his arms, and leafed through two other options of protest, one saying 'IMPOSSIBLE', he chose the remaining one which said 'TELL THE TRUTH" Like a shot it too went up in protest, Edgar shaking his head slowly in silent disbelief.

And so the sermon went. Edgar flipping up two more 'YOU'RE LYING's and one more 'IMPOSSIBLE' in the thirty minute sermon. Michael leaning back in disappointment, knowing that the police would be waiting for him outside.

Descending the lectern, the priest then took a back seat, seemingly oblivious to the visual comment of a distant parishioner. The ceremony continued, ended quietly, and they waited quietly as all of the others shuffled out.

Edgar looked exhausted, his eyes staring at a distant object located as near as his knees. Not saying anything more, he slipped the cardboard signs back under his coat. They then rose, grabbed their satchels and closed in behind the last of the crowd.

As they solemnly passed through the doors and out onto the street, Michael saw the priest greeting the parishioners one by one, exchanging some smiles, a warm handshake, and a gentle laugh.

Michael looked for a getaway, an angle around the priest, using the crowd as a shield, but was shocked again as Edgar pushed his way into the lineup, to be the next one. Suddenly face to face, Edgar blurted out what he tried to say with his signs.

"You must stop lying to people. You're giving then false hope and faith."

For a second, the priest stood there quietly calibrating; assessing.

He then broke into a welcoming smile, extending his arms and placing them firmly on Edgar's shoulders.

"Edgar,. It is so good to see you."

Michael was taken aback, and stood slightly out of place and he watched two seemingly old friends meet.

Edgar was speechless, but not surprised.

"How are you doing?" the priest pressed.

"I'm okay." Edgar responded meekly, but in a beat, he regained his bravado. "Listen, you must stop lying to these people."

"About what?" the priest asked, stepping back and folding his arms in a gently cradle.

"That God loves us, that he cares for us, that everything he does is for our own good."

The priest listened patiently, and replied with a shocking defense.

"But he does Edgar, he does…" the priest gauged down his voice. "I understand your pain Edgar. I know the loss you have suffered. It's heartbreaking and a pain that is seemingly endless. But there is an end. Part of which is the giving from us. Your spiritual family."

Edgar was flushed, motionless in listening.

The priest then took the silence as an opening and placed his hand on Edgar's shoulder. "We are always here when you need us." He then glanced over at Michael, "Introduce me to your friend." he said as a way to break the tension.

Edgar turned sheepishly, "This is….

"Jeff!" Michael said, reaching forward and shaking the priest's hand. "I enjoyed your sermon." He added quickly.

"Wonderful!" the priest exclaimed smiling broadly at the obvious patronization. "Perhaps both of you again next week?" he asked in a motion to move the line along.

Edgar just shook his head, mumbled something unintelligible and the two of them walked away and down the wide steps.

Halfway down a stooped woman wearing an overly insulated coat stood watching and listening to the whole affair. She didn't smile, but seemed enraptured by the two of them, staring intently as they walked down the steps.

"You're being an asshole." She suddenly blurted out through overdrawn lipstick and wrinkled pink-rouged cheeks.

"Leave me alone Mrs. Flanagan."

"My grandson has been mowing your lawn since you've been gone and you come into god's house and create blasphemy."

"Just pointing out injustices and lies." Edgar said

trying not to to be confrontational, but definitely trying to get the last word.

"Bullshit." She added stamping her cane on the stone. "You're just being an asshole." By now, the two of them were down to sidewalk, just within earshot of her last yelp. "Grow up…. get past it…. People die."

In the walk back to the bus stop, they said nothing. Getting on the bus, equally silent.

"Why don't you go home?' Michael asked.

"She's there."

"Who? Your mom?"

Edgar nodded. "In every room, in every chair, in every mirror."

Michael listened quietly.

"I needed a break. That's why I'm here. I had to get away. Figure out what to do."

Michael looked out the window as the vehicle navigated the traffic and stoplights, and thought deeply for the first time about his kids, and the trials Andrea was going through. He exhaled, stared down at his open hands, then clasped them neatly in his lap.

CHAPTER V

Turning the water off at the kitchen sink, Andrea stood gazing out the window, her hands lying limply on the counter. The children were off on playdates so the house had an unusual quiet, a stillness she was uncertain on how to deal with. The inactivity was unnerving, as she was now faced with the vacancy of a missing partner; with the quiet, the grief and guilt began to creep in; clouding her decisions, skeptical of her own judgement.

"What are you thinking?' Josef asked, he was seated at the kitchen table, a cup of coffee in front of him, his arms folded across his chest in patient anticipation. "I don't understand." She said softly. "I just don't understand Grandpa."

She reached into the cupboard above her, and hooked her finger around a yellow coffee cup with the letters MOM emblazoned across the ceramic. For a moment she hesitated at the sight of the one next to it marked DAD. She closed the cupboard and poured the coffee.

Shuffling over to the table, her oversized t-shirt accentuating her dropped shoulders, she pulled the chair away from the table, pulled up her loose fitting blue sweatpants, and flopped into the chair. For a few moments there was silence as she gazed at the stack of crayon drawings pushed into a pile at the end of the table. Loose crayons; broken and worn down lay around like spent artillery shells. On almost every sheet was stick figure of Michael. Dad playing with the girls, dad fighting the zombies, daddy as an angel.

She pushed a loose lock of hair away from her face, blending in back into the lines leading to her ponytail. She looked at Josef, gave him a tight obligatory smile. Josef stayed silent. He could see she was processing. It would come out in time.

"Is it me? She asked. "Was there something that I'd done that caused him to leave?"

"No." was Josef's quick reply. "I can tell you for certain that it has nothing to do with you."

"Another woman?" She queried.

"Michael isn't the type to throw everything away for a piece of ass."

"Then what Grandpa? What causes a man to leave his wife and kids?"

Josef placed both of his hands on his coffee cup, it still held some warmth, and felt good on his leathered palms.

"I don't care about me," she said, "but my kids…" She now looked directly at him "You know what it is like."

He nodded slowly. "When it happened to me, it was my last day as a boy. In fact, the only time I was considered one was at the refugee camp. My age helped me get a more rations."

He tried to redirect the topic.

"Any news from the detective?"

"He called the other night and wanted to bring over some Chinese food and talk and at first I said ok. But then I called him back and told him no." she took a sip from her cup. "Nothing to really talk about."

Silence.

"I think a lot about the vacations and the times we had together with the kids, and when we first got married, and all the holidays." She hesitated, "I miss that, but what I miss most is him not being here. Next to me, in the same room, driving together, lying next to me in bed." She looked down at the table, tears beginning to well in her eyes. "I miss him so much."

Josef shifted in his seat. He didn't mind sharing his own past, perhaps something could help. "When I was on the freighter coming to America, there were a lot of men that, had a reason to be there. I remember that when we were in port everyone was edgy. There was work to be done and everyone had a part in it, but there was something else. There was always the 'hurry' to get away.

Josef paused and looked out over the kitchen as if seeing something again, a vision that reoccurred in his mind whenever he drew back the curtain and this image was there.

"But when we set sail, and the port vanished with the horizon, everyone relaxed eager for the routine. And as the days went on, the men became who they really were."

He looked at Andrea. "Some men who I never saw drink even a glass of beer in port, drank whisky the whole time. Another just a played his guitar, others wrote, some just sat up on deck and stared out at the sea, deep in thought. One in particular went into his cabin a seaman, and came out a woman."

He slowly laid his hands flat on the table, leaning forward as he did. "The point is they weren't running away from something, they just didn't want to be who they were or at least try and find it with no judgement.

Andrea listened quietly, sniffing on occasion, a tear rolling down here cheek.

"Do you think he'll come back?"

"I think you will see him again." Josef smiled, and grabbed both ofher hands in his own. "In the meantime, you must go forward. If I hadn't I wouldn't be here," and he winked. "and neither would you."

Walking with confidence, Michael crossed the compound and approached Hayden's hut. Without any hesitation, he pushed the flap aside and walked into the center, sitting down deliberately in front of the leader, who calmly set aside the book he was reading and smiled peacefully back.

"How can I help you?' Hayden said with a gracious smile.

Michael fidgeted a little, then began. "So I think I understand how this place works, you know, with everyone contributing and stuff, but I'm not sure what you do."

With one fluid motion, Hayden reached to either side of him and set out four candles, all deeply set in glass jars.: I just listen." Was his response.

"To what?"

"To you."

"To me?"

"To you."

"And what are those for?"

Having set out the candles in a line between them, he reached behind him and pulled out a long necked butane lighter.

"These are for you'"

"For me?"

Hayden stopped for a second to break the redundancy. "For you."

"Each one of these represents an emotion." After lighting them all, he returned the lighter to his back pocket and folded his hands in his lap. "The red candle represents anger, the green one is for joy, the yellow one is for fear, and the blue one is for sadness."

He stopped and looked at Michael.

"How do you feel?"

"Uhh,,,,"

"Are you ready to go home?"

Michael wasn't sure how to answer.

"No." he began.

Silence. An uncomfortable silence, where Michael at a certain point, felt he had to say something. "I'm scared to go home."

Again silence.

"There are some things I've done that I can't go back to."

Silence. And so it went on for about 15 minutes, until

Michael began to get frustrated and as it was evident to Hayden, wanted to get out.

"I'm finished." He concluded as he struggled to get up. Hayden then reached beside him into a long box and took out a long thin piece of thread. He blew out the candles, then pulled out a yellow bead from a box hidden next to him. Sliding it on, it balanced itself in the middle of the string.

"This is yours. Keep it, and when you come back, we will add more as we progress."

"Why yellow?"

"It's based on what you've told me."

Smiling, he then returned to his book, now oblivious to the man slowly rising and exiting the hut.

A little dazed, Michael almost stumbled into Dr. Coda.

"There you are Michael?' he exclaimed, obviously glad to see him. "Excellent, I see you have had a talk with Hayden."

Michael wasn't sure, and displayed his string like a preschooler with his first 'mat' project.

"I see," Dr. Coda said, taking the vial from Michael and holding it up to the sun. "It's 'Fear' today, not unusual."

As he raised the string, his sleeve fell back and Michael could see the colored bands on his wrist with the numbers. "Don't lose this." The Dr. replied, as he gave the string back to Michael, where upon he slipped his necklace over his head.

"Now come with me and I will set you up with your tasks today."

Once again Michael was walking quickly behind the stride of a driven man. They disappeared down a shaded path at a far end of the compound, that quickly sloped downward and away from the huts.

"I understand you were successful with Edgar on his routes yesterday."

"Yea..." he answered.

"How did it go?"

"Fine, except for the church. Not sure why we stopped there."

"Edgar is still angry. But he's working his way through it. He doesn't realize it, but he is doing better. When I found him living under a bridge by the highway, he was much worse. When it is time for him to leave, he'll be ready."

"Okay. Anyway the other weed drops went okay. Pretty simple if you ask me?"

Dr. Coda stopped and looked quizzically at Michael. "Weed drops?' He offered in an odd way as if suddenly learning a new language. "Do you think this is marijuana?"

"Well yea. What else would it be?"

The Dr. began walking again, his head turned slightly in comprehension. "You'll soon see." At which point they turned at a bend in the path, and there before him stretched the answer.

As they exited the woods they came to the edge of a large seemingly endless meadow. Stretching before him were huge expanses of colorful plants flowering in different shades of yellow and purple, orange and red. An expanse of endless and oddly organized plots, with a few people scattered around tending them plots with hoes and scythes.

"This is Truman's Glen." The doctor stated as they approached a narrow paved road which runs past the plots, a sidewalk connecting the plots to the road. "This was planned as a subdivision in the late 70's, but the developers disappeared and it fell into bankruptcy before a single home had been built." Michael gazed around somewhat dumbfounded at the long paved streets, cracked with tall weeds. All of the basic foundations of a subdivision were there; curbs, sidewalks, and dozens of poured foundations. Looking up, he could see rusted street signs, black lettering on white backgrounds in an archaic design. 'Kennedy Ave.' and 'Johnson Street' detailed directions and homes with no addresses.

As they walked down the street, Michael could see where poured foundations designed for basements and floor boards were now growing plots for single varieties of perennials. Some even had small shrubs in neat, weed free rows with lavender berries. "When the Forest Preserve expanded, this area was deemed too much of a natural resource to lose to development, so it was annexed and quickly forgotten, that is until we decided to use it for our own needs."

"Which are?"

"Herb mixes designed to control pain. As if on cue, the grower Tony Wong walked over, smiling broadly. "see you brought another strong back."

"Mr. Wong here has a recipe which consists of using

select varieties of plants in specific quantities to alleviate pain."

"Why don't you just market and sell it and get rich."

Mr. Wong interjected suddenly sporting a solemn face. "Some of these varieties could be considered in the family of Opiates. Plus, none are native, have to keep them under control. Once the government gets into it, our mission will be stifled.

"So we use this as a work farm for people like yourself; people looking for a second chance, and an opportunity to provide for the common good." Dr. Coda concluded. "We need some supplies to keep the compound functioning, so we use it to barter. Mostly retirement homes and a few health food stores." He leaned forward as if assuming was eavesdropping. "People we can trust to keep quiet about this place."

Mr. Wong was quick to return to his mission. "Come with me and I will set you up with what needs to be done." Taking that as his cue, Dr. Coda nodded and patted Michael on the shoulder as if saying good luck.

As the diminutive young man headed off, Michael turned to follow him. While they walked down the empty street, Michael could see a half dozen people already trimming plants and weeding lots. Off to the left, he noticed the girl he had seen the other day. With her hair pulled back into a tight ponytail, and a baseball hat pulled low over her eyes, her lean frame seemed oddly askew as she bent over at the waist instead of the knees. As if on cue, she straightened up and faced the two of them walking passed her lot. Michael gave her a slow wave; she nodded in reply, brushed her nose with the back of her gloves, then bent over to return to her work.

Reaching a lot walled in by a raised concrete foundation, there was a set of pruners, some large leather gloves and a heavy burlap bag with a leather strap.

"Real simple today, you are in the Echinacea lot," Mr. Wong clapped his hands loudly as if bringing the plants to attention. "These plants are done flowering, and the heads have dried up so now is the time to harvest them before they dry further and the seeds drop."

Picking up easily on the expectations, Michael slipped on the gloves and slung the strip over his shoulder, all the while watching the girl in the next lot bending over her own assigned space.

Peter had just entered his office when a technician poked his head around the corner of the doorway. "Got a second." He asked.

Pater gazed at his desktop, looking for a reason not to. Not finding one, he acquiesced. "Sure."

The two walked a short distance to an open cubicle where the technician had a frozen image of the parking lot of the restaurant on the monitor.

"With regards to your missing person, I checked the store that owned the semis and they had a security camera on the trailers. It doesn't show the restaurant, and it is on the other side of the trailers, so you can't see anything between the restaurant and the last trailer…"

"So what's your point?"

Taken aback slightly, the technician continued "uh….

Well, watch while I run a loop." He clicked and the camera shook from the initial explosion, then filmed steadily a the silent immovable trailers.

Clicking the trailer film off, he looked at Peter. "Did you see it?"

With a sullen mumble, Peter uttered "No." Arrowing back to the beginning of the tape, the technician pointed to the top of a copse of trees rising above the last trailer. Again the explosion, then silence, then the top of the trees parted slightly for a few seconds, a Few moments later, it opened again.

"Your boy went into the woods and didn't come back."

"Ok." Peter replied. Peter raised his head, intrigued. "Then why did the trees part twice?"

"It would part twice if someone came through and picked him up and then went back into the woods. "The technician smiled at his conclusion.

"So someone was waiting for him?"

The technician shrugged. "Perhaps. I'm just showing you what I saw. You're the detective you have to figure it out from here."

Peter exhaled, almost in a fit of exhaustion at the sudden burden of new evidence.

"You ok?" the tech. asked.

"Yes, I'm okay. Just a little distracted. "Saw my dad yesterday and….uh, just processing some things."

The tech. smiled openly, a fresh wall to write a confession on.

"We have a contentious relationship," Peter added,

"and I spend hours after talking to him wondering if by trying not to be him, I am becoming him."

"The curse of the prodigal son." The tech. added. "Listen, I don't know your situation or your past, but if you want a little advice from someone whose job it is to study behavior, it's hard to change. If you think you're going in one direction. Check your motives because that is what you're going to base your choices on."

Peter didn't say anything and just digested what the tech. said.

"Look," he continued. "Does your dad live on his own? Does he need you for anything?"

"No. Not really. He lives by himself at the Manchester Arms. Downtown."

The tech. raised his eyebrows. "Wow, he has done well. Great place to live."

"Yeah, he made some good investments."

"Well that makes it a little easier. At least he doesn't truly need anything from you."

"But it's always hard to talk to him without fielding questions about the choices Ive made."

"'That's the layer of guilt that all parents lay on. I could go on for hours about what my parents think, not to mention what my brothers and sister want. They get pissed off when they ask if I'm bringing anyone for X-mas and I tell them 'Yah…brandy.' I think they are finally getting it."

"I know what you mean." Peter said to finish the conversation. "Hey, listen; save that film to a file and send me a link. I want to go over it a while, see if I can pick up anything else."

"Sure thing." The tech. turned back to his computer while Peter walked back to his office. Rather than sit down, he stood behind the desk and gazed at the mounds of files stacked in front of him. Taking a deep breath, he reached into his top right drawer and looked down at a portrait picture of a woman in her late twenties with long blond hair, a bright yellow sweater and a calm smile with hopeful eyes. After a few moments he slowly closed the drawer, walked over to the clear window, and wondered.

In the field at lunch time, Michael met with all of the others, about a half dozen, and meet at a cul-de-sac at the end of Carter Circle. In the center, Mr. Wong was handing out sandwiches and bottled water, and each took their allotment and settled down as one large group.

After Michael had found a comfortable place on a raised curb, the young girl strode over leisurely and sat across from him. Two other men soon followed.

"You're new." She said in a surprisingly low, coarse voice.

"'Bout a week." He replied. "you?"

"Couple of months." Now that they were conversing he had a chance to study her. She was a few years younger then him, with thin strands of brown hair slipping out of her knit cap. By her complexion he could tell she had been in the elements for some time. Her skin was a ruddy brown, and her clothes were showing the wear of the outdoors, but she seemed pleasant and it was someone new to talk to other than Dr. Coda and Edgar.

"My name's Julia." She said.

"Michael." He replied.

"How did you get here?" Michael continued, biting into the ham and cheese sandwich as he waited for the reply.

"Dr. Coda found me. I was trying to sneak into a YWCA for the night, and he made me a better offer."

When she bit into her sandwich, Michael could see lettering on her fingers. At first he just thought they were just the errant Chinese lettering that tattoo artists try to con their customers into adding, but in a fine calligraphy he could now make out very detailed letters.

"What's with the lettering?" He asked.

With a mouthful of food, she placed her sandwich in her lap, made two fists, and turned them towards Michael so he could read them. Between the middle and outer knuckle, on the fingers on her left hand, he could see a single letter on each D O N T; and on the right he could see D O I T. Together the fingers supplied advice either for or against.

"The letters help me decide, sometimes a visual can help."

"I bet." Was all Michael could really add. By now another boy had joined the two of them in conversation. He had the appearance of someone who had also been outdoors for awhile, yet he still had the feral dog look of a young man, with the leanness of an athlete.

"Daniel here, he has a more interesting tattoo." She remarked grinning and taking a bite of her sandwich.

"Very funny." Daniel answered with a slow drawl.

"Just saying." She added.

"So do you do this everyday?" Michael asked to no one in particular.

"Pretty much." Daniel answered. The girl shrugged.

"Mostly it's not a job, you come when you want. But it's really relaxing to me." Julia added. "It's quiet here and there is time to think."

"Music would be better." Daniel chirped up, then grinned slyly and dug into his sandwich.

"I don't think so," Julia angrily shot back.

"Why not?" Michael queried.

"He knows I have chromesthesia."

"A what?" he asked

"I see colors when I hear certain instruments. With me I see yellow when I hear guitar music."

"I've never heard that before." "It's rare. but It happens to me."

"Actually she's crazy." Daniel spoke out again, baiting her as he took another bite of his sandwich.

Now she was quiet, frustration building. "That's not true." She said in a deep voice. 'DOIT' flexing into a fist, 'DON'T' lay flat and at a glance.

"Why are you here?' Michael asked trying to take some of the tension out of the air.

"I'm here because my mom thinks I am crazy, and when I tell her, she just turns away and ignores me, like I'm making this up. I see what I see." She exhaled, grabbed her sandwich with both hands, and began to eat again.

"So you left because she thought you were crazy?"

"No, I left because no one believed me. And I

left because my mom's boyfriend decided I was more interesting than her and that getting in the shower with me was his way of getting to know me better. When he stepped in, I stepped out."

She now looked up directly at Michael, her gaze sharp and inquisitive.

"You're turn." She replied, pointing a tattooed finger in his direction.

Michael thought for a second

"Guess I needed a break. Lots of things coming at me, wife, little kids, job." Deciding not to mention the debts owed and the collectors that were surely out looking for him, he stopped and gave a weak smile. "Needed to get away." Was his last comment.

Not sure whether to believe him a if there was something he was omitting, Julia and Daniel both nodded in kind.

"How about you?" Michael asked Daniel so as to complete the circle of confession.

"Couldn't stop fighting." Daniel said shaking his head slowly. "I just kept getting angry and arguing, and that lead to fights, most of them I couldn't win."

As Daniel spoke, Michael scanned over his face and he could now see the scars and cuts from dozens of blows. "It's quiet here, nobody gives me any problems."

Without any further conversation, Mr. Wong seemingly out of nowhere appeared and prompted them to go back to work. Daniel headed off in one direction while Julia and Michael headed off towards their lots which were close together.

"Have you talked to Hayden yet?" she asked.

"Yes, I saw him this morning for the first time. He doesn't' say much."

"Never does, at least to me. All he seems to do is listen."

"How many bead do you have?"

"I'm very close to being done. Started out with lots of greens and reds, different colors now as I get closer to the ends."

Michael nodded, as he approached his lot. "Don't work too hard." as he hitched his bag higher on his shoulder.

"Never do." She replied with a sly smile as Michael watched her walk away.

The day was misty, cool. Unusual for this time of year and when Josef stepped off the bus, he pulled the lapels around his neck to protect his neck and pulled the fedora down a little further over his brow.

He hesitated in front of the cemetery, not sure whether to enter. He paused long enough for the bus to pull away, forcing him to commit to walking through the tall limestone pillars and onto the rolling lawn. The black steel gates that closed the cemetery at night, were wide open, and a slow procession of five cars were slowly passing by, heading out of the cemetery through the gates. As he walked along the sidewalk that led to lot A15-14, located on a small knoll behind a thin copse of trees, he scanned the open horizon, relieved that there were no funerals today. When he visited and there were, he always felt awkward, an intruder prowling around a private moment.

But today, there were only the birds and the headstones and he strode past one after another of the familiar ones. Most were flat lot stones, essentially a door stopper, but further out in the older lots he could see taller more elaborate monuments, some were broken obelisks, dedicated to a life interrupted. Others more of a final, ornate, ego message for the ages. They were like majestic oaks among scrub, as large in death as they viewed themselves in life.

Walking down the central path, he saw all the usual names, more familiar to him in death than they ever could in life. For almost five years, they had greeted him and led him to where Gloria lay.

With a tight bundle of yellow carnations, in his hands, wrapped in protective plastic, he felt himself smiling as he drew near. It took years before he could accept that she was here, but the conformity and permanence grew comfortable and eventually settled into acceptance as time passed. He would joke that it took this long for her to learn to listen. And listen she did.

He saw the familiar granite headstone, and proceeded up the shallow hill. On clear warm days, he would bring a fine bottle of German red wine, pouring a little over the grave as he poured his own glass. Lying next to her on the grass, watching the clouds fly away.

But today he would lay down his flowers, stand obediently and just talk.

Looking down at the grave, he laid the flowers by the

stone, and bowed his head, his hands deep in his pockets, hat low over his brow.

"My dear Gloria." He began softly. "You look well. I'm doing okay." He continued in German.

"Not much on my end, although Randolph has decided to return to the homeland. He feels his work here is done and he wants to go back. He still has a sister there and he can stay with her and with his boys grown and his wife gone, not much left for him to do here. Guess he decided now was the time for him to do something for himself."

"With the badness of Michael's situation, I have been thinking myself. Our daughter Cynthia and the cheap bastard she married have a stronger relationship now with Andrea. I've given all the support I can do, I think it's time for me to fade back a little."

He stopped now, a cool wind crossed the lawn and sent a chill down his spine. He chuckled 'Someone walked over my grave' as the old saying goes, nowhere else to prove it other than here."

"As time goes by", he continued "I think about going back. The same is for Randolph as for me. With you gone and the girl managing ok, perhaps it is time for me to look at where I want to be. It's not just Randolph, everything is changing. The things we always knew are fading away, perhaps I should too."

He placed the flowers on the grave, and stood silently in the afternoon sun. "You are my heart, you always will be, and I won't be gone forever, but I think I should do this. I hope you understand."

With that statement, he wiped away a tear and brushed his nose. "I will be back." he promised. Then softly turned and walked back towards the gate.

Peter met the Ranger at the Park District headquarters. It was a brand new facility, small yet modernized. A learning center was behind the office itself with a small museum equipped with stuffed native species and a large wall map depicting the topography and the location of unique landmarks the visitors could walk or bike to.

Crossing the midnight black parking lot with fresh yellow parking lines, he smiled at buildings in a faux-log cabin style construction, very different from the warehouse - sweat box atmosphere of the early buildings.

Walking into the small entryway and then into the waiting area, he forced a rather plump brunette with thick glasses and piles of papers all around the top of the desk.

"Are you Detective Bachman?" she enquired in a rather rough voice and a distant look.

"Yes, I believe the ranger is expecting me."

She turned her head as if to cough and directed her voice towards an open door leading to a back office.

"Police are here!" she bellowed.

"Be right there" was the muffled reply.

"He'll be right here." She repeated.

"Just finishing up a quick report." He added.

"He's finishing a report right now." She echoed.

"Ask him if he wants coffee or something."

"He wants to know if you want coffee or something?"

Peter looked over to a small card table set up against

the wall with a stained glass coffee pot holding a quarter of a port of tar like liquid. An open aluminum tray was filled with a half -eaten Danish, small Styrofoam plates and a small collection of plastic forks and knives – handle end up – placed in an aged coffee cup. He noticed it had been visited often, just by looking at the disheveled stack of napkins and scattered crumbs across the table's surface.

"No thanks." He replied.

"He said 'No thanks'" she passed on.

"Ok." Was the reply

"That's ok." She responded.

After Peter stood for only a few moments, the ranger suddenly appeared in the doorway in full uniform with a tight haircut and a smile of perfectly equal teeth.

"Send him back now." The ranger replied.

"You can go back there now." The secretary said as Peter walked around her desk and headed into the office.

Shaking hands, they each reached for chairs, the rangers behind the desk, the detective in a plush swivel chair in the corner. Before he sat down, the ranger motioned for Peter to close the door, which Peter did obediently, then watched as the ranger struggled to get behind his desk. Peter noticed that the ranger's chair was cushioned, and adjusted to a peculiar angle.

"Bad back?' he asked.

The ranger nodded. "About 10 years ago I had climbed a tree to view an owl's nest. We were sure she was gone, but she was closer than we thought. I heard the warning over the radio, and in my hurry to get out of the tree I slipped and fell about 20 feet. Duff on the ground was thick enough to cushion my fall so I didn't break anything, but I really wrenched the spine. It has never been the same."

"A lot of pain?"

He shrugged "I'm on some pretty good stuff. Don't really feel it, just awkward to move now." He smiled politely "So I saw the video you sent me. I sent a few rangers over there yesterday and I went with them." He grimaced and shook his head. "Nothing there. No trails, no broken branches, no bodies."

"How far in the woods did you go?"

"A few hundred yards. Brush is pretty thick in that area. Canopy is dense also so any air surveillance would be difficult."

Peter sat there quietly for a few moments.

Reaching into a manila folder on his desk, the ranger pulled out a detailed map of the park. With a red pen, he put an X at the corner of the border of the park.

"Here is where you said you saw the movement." Using the pen as a pointer, he whirled it in a slow circle. "This is 2500 acres. He could have come out at any of these points, or gone into the center where we only go about twice a year.

"Basically he could be anywhere." Peter said finishing the thought.

The ranger nodded, giving him the map. He shrugged to make a final statement.

Peter gazed at the map, trying to absorb the magnitude of the size of the park. Hundreds of acres were divided into chunks of ecosystems named after politicians, war heroes, and prominent donors.

"Truman's Glen." The detective stated aloud. The ranger suddenly became still.

Peter smiled. "I remember when I was a kid the ghost stories about the place. Open graves and voices."

The ranger answered. "Big dreams." He smiled weakly. "Sorry I couldn't help you."

Peter shrugged. "It was a long shot. Thanks again." He rose, the ranger struggling to rise to see him out.

"Don't bother." Peter replied, shook the ranger's hand, then proceeded out of the office and back onto the parking lot.

Waiting for the outer door to close, the ranger reached into his breast pocket and took out a small cell phone. Holding it close to his face, he texted into it; "A wolf is sniffing at the door." He typed. Hesitating, he pushed send, then leaned back into his chair to take the pressure off his lower back.

CHAPTER VI

Peter took a deep breath and exhaled it slowly while staring at the blank screen of his cell phone. He moved his hand around awkwardly to get comfortably while making a fist with his left hand and releasing it slowly.

Finally, with his confidence at a peak, he swiped the screen, revealed the dial pad, then hit favorites and pushed the call button at Andrea's' name. Bringing the phone to his ear, he moved some post-it notes a few inches, rearranged the three pens on his desk and gave a swipe over the open section of his desk directly in front of him with his open hand. The phone rang twice, then Andrea picked up.

"Hi detective." She said with a distracted tone.

"Do you have second?" he asked. Now suddenly bowing his head down at his desk, concentrating now on this important conversation, and also the small pinhole in his desk blotter. "Sure." She said with a hitch in her voice. "Just cleaning up some games after the kids, 'cleaned up' the games."

"Good. Well…ah…we have a lead in your husband's case."

He could hear the rustling in the background stop with the silence.

"We believe…" he continued. "he disappeared into the forest preserve at the end of the parking lot."

"Really." She said breathlessly. "Is this a real thing or are you guessing?"

"We are fairly certain that this is something….that… ahh…we are going to pursue."

"So for sure he is alive?'

"We won't know that until we find him, but it is a possibility Ther is something there. But our next question is, is he alone."

"What do you mean." She said suddenly getting defensive.

"Well, it is just a theory, but it seems he was injured."

She gasped on the other end of the phone.

But not apparently seriously, as he was able to walk away from the explosion, but badly enough that he needed assistance going further."

"I see." She said.

"Listen… ahh… he said as he began his pitch. "… do you have time to meet and we can go over some ideas."

"What kind of ideas?'

"I need more information about who your husband hung around with. We have to assume that there is some sort of plot or was it just a friend helping him out. Perhaps someone else in the restaurant at the same time."

Silence.

"I don't think there is much more I can tell you."

"Perhaps, but just in talking there could be something new uncovered. Some new clue that gets scratched out."

"I... uh... I really don't think there is anything new."

He began to reach now. Anything to get face to face with her. On that point he knew he had the chance to get closer. Get a little nearer, maybe have the chance for her to see what he had to offer. Then, just maybe.

"You can bring the kids if you like." He blurted out, then winced at the obvious over reach. It felt like almost a plea.

"Look, I don't feel comfortable with this, in fact I get the sense that this is a more personal effort than professional."

Peter pursed his lips, leaned back in his chair, and placed his left arm behind his head with an expression similar to a missed basketball shot.

"I'm sure you are a great guy, but I have a lot to process right now. A lot to....uh... cope with. God, I don't even know if my husband is alive or dead, so for right now, please just concentrate on answering that question for me."

It was Peter's turn to be silent. "I understand." He replies rather meekly. "I'm sorry if I gave that impression." He answered. "Finding your husband is all I'm focused on right now. If that came off as insensitive and personal, please understand it wasn't meant to be that."

"Okay." She added firmly.

This conversation was over.

"Either way, if you think of something new, please don't hesitate to call me. Anytime."

"I understand." She added and hung up.

He didn't click the phone off, just watched the screen phase out from connected to call ended. A curtain slowly descending to finish the act.

He set the phone flat on the desk, and stared at it for some time. Deep in his mind he began to scroll through the facts of his life. Career versus marriage, family versus comrades, working all hours versus home after eight. His hope diminished as the facts of his situation appeared like odd tree stumps rising out of a draining lake.

"Get real." He said, then turned to the pile of manila folders on his desk.

Michael entered the hut this particular morning more determined than ever. He sat down heavily in front of Hayden, crossed his legs forcefully, and looked at the leader with a stern look.

"You have something on your mind." Hayden replied, closing a notebook and setting it next to him so he could concentrate fully on the young man in front of him. As Michael began to talk, Hayden reached for the lighter next to him and let the candles already set out in front of him.

"I'm trying to understand what is going on here. So for it seems we are selling….."

"Bartering." Hayden interjected.

"Bartering." Michael accepted the change. "this mythical pain killing 'weed' for materials outside of the camp."

"Ok." Hayden added.

"So what's in it for you if there is no money coming in?"

""Have you ever heard of the Templar Knights?"

Michael hesitated. "Farm system hockey team?"

"No." Hayden said sharply. "Briefly so as not to confuse you; the Templar Knights were an organization formed in the Middle Ages to protect the Catholic church's acquisitions in the Middle East in addition to looking for the Holy Grail."

Michael thought for second, then snapped his fingers. "Indiana Jones…. The third movie."

Hayden hesitated. "Actually the first, but let's go with that. Anyway, after a period of time the hierarchy of the church viewed them as a threat and had the whole organization arrested and disbanded."

"What does that have to do with anything?"

"Because man of the royal families in your disagreed with this action and hid many of the knights and their leaders, which in time created a secret society on their own. By reestablishing themselves in an underground organization that instead of fronting the Christian good of resettling the Holy Land, they dedicated themselves to service and compassion. At times they were giving sanctuary to anyone who requested it or need the step forward."

"So everyone here is a knight?"

"No, not at all, we are not a religious organization, but my desire is to create a similar model, offering a step, a hope if you want to call it that is away from all the distractions of society."

"I've seen you turn a lot of people away."

"Dr. Coda and I only accept the people we feel we can help."

"There was a girl this morning they turned away. She looked terrible, no teeth, skinny, her eyes were really small."

"She's an addict. She is too far gone. "She has what I all the 'look of need'. The only instinct she has left is to get high. To find drugs to get high to get to the mindset she craves."

Michael was quiet. "What about me?"

Hayden leaned back, placing his hands on his knees. "What about you?"

Michael now felt the door of honesty swing a little wider.

"They are looking for me." He confessed.

"Who? The police?"

"Perhaps the police. Someone else that that ....I owe."

"I see."

"Not sure how to go back while they are looking for me. Let's just say it won't end well."

Hayden was back to form now, listening patiently, observing his movements and actions, nodding in understanding when needed.

"I mean…it's a money thing. A big one, one that I am ashamed of. Something that could really screw up my marriage and my kids and everything else."

He looked down at the floor. "I already lost my job over it. I didn't want to lose my wife too. But I really miss her and the kids."

There was now a long moment of silence between them as Michael disappeared deep into thought.

"I can't believe I did such a stupid thing. To put everything at risk."

He looked at Hayden with a helpless look. "I can't believe I was so selfish."

Hayden could only nod, then turned his hands so his palms faced upwards. For a few more moments Michael sat there, then slowly rose to his feet, pulling out the necklace hidden under his shirt. Hayden offered him a large jar with multicolored beads. Pulling out a blue one he slid it over the string it was his first marking sadness.

Julia and Daniel were together, tasked with unloading the cart and emptying the bags of herbs into the appropriate bins. Together they had moved the cart to the edge of the field, where huge bins were set up to accommodate the storage of the herbs. Some contained roots and dried leaves, while smaller ones contained the seeds. They worked in silence until Daniel suddenly threw down an empty bag after dumping it into a bin.

"You like him!!" he declared.

Taken aback, Julia stood silent and rigid.

"Who?" she replied softly, trying to take the edge off of a suddenly confrontational situation.

"You know who, that new guy, whatever his name is."

"You mean Michael? Yes, he's okay I guess."

"But I've seen how you look at him."

A bit bewildered, she shook her head slowly in disbelief. "Not sure what you're talking about." she stated dismissively and returned to her work unloading the cart. Daniel took a step closer, "Stop screwing around with me, you want to be with him right?"

She stopped and turned to face him again. "Look, I don't know what you are talking about. Yea, he's a nice guy but that's all. Just somebody new to talk to."

"Like I'm not enough, I thought we were… you know, close."

"We work in the fields together, Daniel, that's not close." Now she was angry. She could feel it rising and wanted to lash out, but instead looked down at the letters on her fingers, the solid ink showing plainly through the dirt from the field.

"My bad." Daniel said indignantly. "Guess I misread it. Maybe I'm blinded by all of these colors only I can see. Maybe that makes me a little crazy."

Now it was her turn to threw the bag into the back of the cart and take a step towards her antagonist. "Listen asshole, I'm fine with who I am. You're the one with the mental problems. Do I like him, sure! Do you know why? He's an adult, not a pathetic child like you!"

"That's it!!" came a strong voice suddenly appearing beside them. "No more!" Mr. Wong finished.

"But he…." Julia began.

"I know, I saw it all, Daniel that's enough for today, head back to camp and I will finish your work. Be ready for work again early tomorrow."

With a scowl, Daniel placed his hands on his hips and walked away from the two of them.

"Thanks Mr. Wong."

"No problem," then he turned to her and replied sternly. "but if there is something between you and Michael, that could be a problem here. Someone may have to leave."

"I understand." She replied, loosening her fists which she had unknowingly formed. She smiled weakly as Mr. Wong began emptying the gags in the appropriate bins, while she resumed what she was doing and wondered.

Josef walked into the bar, a thick manila folder under his arm. Assuming his place at the round table with his pint of beer and the usual suspects in their places, which was encouraging in that no one was missing at their advanced ages.

Sitting down roughly, he eagerly opened the envelope and spilled out collections of photos. The visual aids halted the conversation as the attendees slowly collected them, and scanned the photographs intently, passing them on only when they had fully ingested everything in the picture.

"The technology available now is amazing." He began as new fresh photos entered old bent and scarred hands.

"There are pictures of our hometowns and how they are now. Compare these to the war photos of the bombing runs and you can see the new Germany that rose up."

Josef reached into the envelope and pulled out a separate stack of photos. Cautiously he handed them to Rudolph.

"I searched for the address you gave me and here are photos of your new home."

Rudolph was a little shocked, but nodded his head knowingly as he glanced through them.

The talking began again slowly as a low hum, then comparisons of where the old was and where the new is now began to amuse them. Josef leaned low over to Rudolph, grinning as he pointed at the photos, placing the pictures back into their own neat pile.

"These are wonderful." Rudolph said with a contented look on his face.

"I'm thinking about what you're doing…you know, going back and everything." Josef confessed. "I'm thinking it would be worth a visit. To see what's there now, maybe visiting some places that survived – like me."

"It would be good for your soul." Rudolph responded. "Would you like to come back with me?"

"No, that's great,: Josef replied, "but no I need to make this journey on my own."

"Are you looking for something?"

"Yes." Josef replied. "A glimpse of my heritage. I want to be back where I grew up…if even for a few days, or maybe a week."

He paused, leaned back in his chair and crossed his arms as he thought deeply.

"I left there a very young man, and given the choice of staying in a desolate, and broken land or choosing to go to a new one to make my future, I chose to come here. I don't regret that. I love being in America. I love being an American." Out of the corner of his eye, he could see the other members of the group silently listening, nodding occasionally in agreement.

"But I was also broken in here." Tapping his chest. "… and I realize that I need something more. Before I pass on, I want to breathe the air there again. I want to see a robust city with cars and new buildings and children playing in the streets. Because in seeing that what's in here will finally be healed."

Rudolph patted him softly on the back. "I understand." He said softly. Unknowingly, Josef rested his hand on his lap, across the front pocket where his melted spoon rested.

Returning to the photos, they all began to chatter jovially and with vigor. Josef pulled out his stack of pictures and showed him where his house was along with his father's mill, his aunt's house, and the spot where he dug himself out of the piano teacher's basement.

After a few hours, Josef checked his watch then assembled his pictures, giving the others to his friends.

They all thanked him and slowly, very slowly rose to leave and return to thier homes. Rudolph collected his and turned to Josef.

"Was my returning to Europe prompting this?" he asked.

"No, although it did help it along. It was the explosion at the restaurant and walking through the debris that prompted it."

"Were you in in the restaurant?" Rudolph asked concerned.

"No, actually my granddaughters husband was there and I was there to help look for him."

"Was he killed."

"At first we thought so, but now it turns out that he was just missing."

Rudolph thought for a second. "Was your grandson in law Michael Planck? The man they are still looking for?"

Josef nodded. "Just disappeared without a trace."

"Very strange." Rudolph added biting his lip.

Michael returned to his place with the harvesting crew. Having started slow with the actual work, after a few days he had ascended to become a very efficient and thorough harvester. On Michael's first few days, Mr. Wong passed by in the afternoon, spending a little time with him to increase his skills and speed.

Now accomplished; he cleansed out his plot of Leuconimium and dropped of his bag at the front steps of the foundation, then gazed at the other plots to see the other workers doing the same thing, with the exception of Julia who seemed to be lagging behind all of the others. Taking the initiative, he strode over to where she was and began to snap the heads off of the flowers and shove them in her bag. A little shocked, she looked up a little dazed, then bent over and worked faster.

"You don't have to help me." She said, her arms suddenly working like pistons, shoving handfuls of seeds in the bag.

"Just lending a hand." He replied. "You would do it for me."

They were able to push through the last quarter of the plot in record time. Helping her tie up and carry her bag to the entrance of the foundation, he threw the bag over his shoulder and walked beside him as she took off her gloves and clapped them together to knock off the dust and dead leaves.

"Just wondering, but have you ever tried this stuff?"

"No." she replied quickly and with a chuckle. "Not my thing."

"Then how does anyone know this stuff works?"

"Dr. Coda is the judge."

She turned to him as they stopped at the sidewalk. "He needs the stuff."

Michael looked at her perplexed. Responding to it, "He's dying of cancer. Didn't you know?" she added.

Michael shook his head slowly. "Never knew it." He replied.

"Yea, the tattoo bands on his wrist….that's his escape plan."

"What's that supposed to mean?"

She shrugged. "That's just what he says."

As he was processing it, Daniel strode over and the three of them began to collect the bags and place them in a small 2-wheeled cart.

Having progressed about a dozen feet into the forest with Daniel in the lead Julia in the center and Michaels behind. Julia threw out a line of conversation.

"I don't believe you." She began

"Who me?' Michael asked.

"There is something else. A guy can leave his wife, but a dad can't leave his kids. You left for another reason."

There was silence as they progressed up the path His

thoughts fell back to his simple basic instinct – who could he trust.

"Money." He offered.

"What about it?'

"I owe some money to some people who are very anxious to get it back."

The trio stopped at a small space in the steep path to catch their breath.

"Not smart." She replied, wiping her mouth with the back of her hand, then pulled her hat down snug over her head.

"How are you going to get out of that mess?' Do you have the money?'

"No. Worse, the interest is pretty steep. I'll never get caught up."

She shook her head while looking at a grinning Daniel. "What is with you men?" She said loud to no one in particular. "You guys always screw up the money."

Having caught their breath, they continued their trek back up to the rise, Michael now sheepishly bringing up in the rear.

Peter entered the Chinese restaurant with the familiarity of an owner. Parting the hanging beads at the doorway, he strode past the smiling young Asian woman attending the register, she nodded in recognition and then walked to a corner booth in the back.

Being a weekday, the restaurant was sparse, which he liked, place is quieter and food comes out faster. Sliding across the plastic seat, he grabbed a trifold menu and perused the Cantonese selections.

Quietly, a waiter slipped in a small plate of egg rolls beside him.

"From the owner." He said softly, then strode over to the next table. Peter smiled. As a beat cop, he was able to break up a small gang that had been terrorizing this neighborhood. The restaurant had a couple of windows broken and hassled some of the customers. Peter 'encouraged' most of them to move on, those that didn't were sent to a juvenile facility up north. None of them returned and the owner never forgot him. Always had a plate for him, on the house.

He was trying to decide between two of his favorites when she slide across from him. He looked up and smiled at her, she returned it readily with the warmth of familiarity.

"Evening detective. Long time no hear." She said pulling her blonde hair back with both hands, then leaning forward with both elbows under her chin in rapt attention. She looked even more stunning than the picture in his drawer taken four years before. Her face was leaner with maturity, eyes brighter, confidence formidable.

"Hi 'beautiful'." He said back to her, setting the menu down on the table having made his choice.

She reached out her hand and he returned the gesture, grasping her fingers tightly in his own. It was then that the diamond on her finger glistened and he winched slightly. "That's new." He offered.

"Happened a couple of days ago. He's a great guy. Accountant."

"Safe business. Happy?"

She beamed "Eternally. Anything new with you?"

He shrugged. "Same thing, different day."

She turned her head slightly "You had a bad experience with a woman."

"You should be a detective."

"Dated one for five years." she shot back. "so is this a pep talk?"

He leaned back, and as if on cue, the waiter appeared. He ordered for both, she added a Cabernet for good measure. He added a Chinese beer.

"It is…" he confessed, when the waiter turned and left. "Feeling a little lonely."

"As your eternal 'friend' she highlighted that work with her fingers, "don't take things so hard. You're a great guy. You'll find the right one."

"Sometimes I wonder."

"Don't wonder. It will happen Don't be in such a hurry. She's out there."

The ego boost continued through the meal but after they both had a few more drinks, the conversation turned.

"What ever happened to us?" he asked.

"History is for Wikipedia. Not going there." She smiled with a hint of fortitude.

"Come on. We were great."

She looked at him directly with suddenly tired eyes, no motion, just the slow turning of the stem of the glass on the table in front of her."

"Do you want to hear it again?" she said sullenly. Peter was quiet, anticipating what was coming through the door he just opened.

"Let's just say you needed to be there. Not one day, not one weekend, not just one night. Every time I brought that up you faded away, deflected it, practicing that talent for evasion you had." She stopped and stared at him hard. "You needed to stop running away."

His silence was telling. The facts now came back to him and the freshness from the lack of committal was palatable.

"I remember." He said softly. "Should have done some things better."

She shrugged and softened the mood with a smile. "The virtue of being friends with an ex girlfriend is that they will always remind you of your faults." she backed off a little. "You will always be my best friend." On that it seemed the dinner was over. As they were gathering their things, the owner stopped by to shake Peter's hand. He was sharp dressed elderly man, tan sport coat with an open collared white shirt. Definitely not someone running a kitchen anymore as Peter knew him in the early days.

"Wonderful meal." Peter complimented him.

"Our pleasure." He replied without a hint of an accent.

Suddenly remembering a fact, Peter asked quickly. "How is your son doing? If I remember right he left the restaurant."

"Yes he did a few years back?" He said with a strong air

of disappointment. "I had hopes that he would step into the management here, but he chose another profession."

"Oh really? What's he doing now?"

"Not sure. Not what I had hoped of course. Something to do with plants. Not sure why he made that choice, but it seems to be something he enjoys."

Peter nodded. "I guess you can't force them to do what you want, it's their path."

Peter stood up and allowed Julia to rise and proceed to the door. "If you see him, Iask him know that if he needs anything, I'm still around. Thank you Peter."

"No problem Mr. Wong."

Edgar, Michael and Daniel existed the bus at the usual spot and the three of them laid down their satchels for bartering while they spent a few moments getting organized.

"Look," Daniel said, "if we split up we will finish faster and get back sooner."

Edgar hesitated.

"I have enough to finish the later part of the route," Daniel added plus there are a few things I need to do, so let's meet back here about 4 and we'll go back together."

"That's fine." Edgar agreed. "That gives us more time also. What about you Michael?"

"Why don't you stay with Edgar." Daniel interjected. "Any objections?"

Michael shrugged. "Ok by me." He said while in the back of his mind he wondered where Edgar would lead him and what level of civil disobedience he will be involved with. Questions like what organization will he piss off today and will he be discovered if they call the police.

"Sounds good." Edgar agreed, and after walking a few blocks, Daniel split off from them and headed towards the downtown. Edgar and Michael proceeded on their assigned route and made the necessary stops at two usual spots, and one new one behind an herbal massage parlor.

Having done their route early, Michael and Edgar then proceeded towards an older part of town the Michael wasn't familiar with.

"Where to?' he asked.

"I need to get a little money to pay the house expenses. I don't live there, but I still have to keep it up, including dropping off a little money to Mrs. Siedrick so she can pay her son. If I don't she'll let the yard go to hell and then I have a real problem."

They walked some distance, until they reached a new, small strip mall with some empty stores, but with a new game shop specializing in video games and gaming systems newly open in the center. With only a few new stores with fresh brick, and its new parking lot, it stood out in this neighborhood of old structures and tired archaic architecture.

Edgar surveyed the scene, looked around the landscape, and seemed to assess the traffic pattern, visibility sight lines and other conditions. Seemingly satisfied, he then went over to the gaming store, walking through the front door with authority, Michael in tow.

"I would like to speak to the manager if he or she is available."

Behind the counter he immediately got the attention of a middle aged bearded man and the young blonde girl standing next to him with a nose ring. They looked up from their inventory sheets and watched this robust, animated figure walking down the aisle towards them.

Reaching the counter, Edgar looked them both over severely, and crossed his arms.

"I'm the manager." The bearded man said.

"I see that you have recently opened and that at this time you may not have the desired clientele to reach the necessary margins required to be successful."

"Possibly. I'm mean, yes, we just opened." The manager said cautiously waiting to see where this was going.

"I have a business proposition for you that will increase the foot traffic through these premises and therefore increase incidental purchases"

The manager now smiled slightly, placing his hands on the counter and confronted Edgar.

"I'm listening." He said.

"As it appears, there are two popular gaming characters that are responsible for the themes of a wide variety of games. I am referring to Lucas the fox and his nemesis Luther the rabbit, a figure that he is always trying to catch."

Michael knew these characters and was familiar with a lot of their games, mainly appealing to young kids, the object being to teach them colors and shapes as they go through the adventures."

"Yes, there are about a half dozen games available with those two characters."

"Good, we have established a market that can be promoted. My proposal is that you supply the costumes of those two characters. My associate and I will stand out front and promote through gesticulation and cadence, a series of encouragements throughout the afternoon to get people to enter these four walls."

"Really." The manager replied flatly, still skeptical.

"Look, as references, call the Patriot Tax agency where I dressed as George Washington for an afternoon and doubled their daily business in a mere four hours. I will also reference the Shakey Hot Dog Shop, actually only a few blocks away, where dressed as the chains mascot where within a mere two hours from 11:00 to 1:00 I was able to populate an empty dining area to the point where people were lined up out the door."

"They are doing better," he turned to look at the girl. "their food is terrible though."

"Bringing my skills to this establishment will give you the notoriety you seek in addition to creating a buzz in the stores in the area that tells them you have 'arrived'." He finished by bracketing the last word with his open palms.

"Why are you so sure?'

Edgar cleaned his throat, and prepared the 'close', He pointed to the north side of the street. "There is a pizza place two blocks down that caters only to children," he pointed to the left. "There is a comic book shop one block down on the corner," and using his thumb he pointed behind him, "and there is a junior high school four blocks away, that has an early dismissal in one hour." He crossed his arms as he finished his pitch. "Not to mention the ice cream shop, pet store, and wing place all within a mile." He raised his finger above his head and turned it in a slow circle to broadcast his zone of concentration.

"This is all good and all, but I don't have the costumes. Sorry."

"Actually there is a costume store behind the appliance store that has these costumes available. At a discount I might add because it is not even near Halloween. Just send the little girl here to get them." He glanced at her briefly. "You're old enough to drive right?"

"Hey!!!" she retorted.

The manager quickly interjected.

"Yes, she can get them, I can call and reserve them. But what do you want?

I can't give you a job."

"I don't want a job. I want $50 for two hours work.

The manager thought for few moments, his nods becoming more pronounced as he made his decision.

"I'm okay with that. I'll pay you the cash and you can advertise out front."

"Well," Edgar chuckled and turned to wink at Michael. "That's fine for me, but I've got a partner."

The young associate returned with the costumes in about ½ an hour. Edgar assumed the title role as the authoritative fox, due to him being the 'closer', while Michael was given the lesser role as the mischievous rabbit. Edgar had a little trouble getting the utility belt on and the hat with the ears through it was ungainly, but he still managed to get the costume assembled then turned to help Michael.

Struggling at first with the suspenders, Michael finally got them adjusted correctly so his overalls weren't pushing his balls up and apart. Now comfortable, he marched around the store get his stride in sync, with the large rabbit feet he was forced to wear. Once adjusted, he then presented the enormous head for Edgar to put on for him.

Cautiously he bent forward, while Edgar slid the plastic rodent face over his head, slightly scrapping an ear as he gently sat it down on Michael's shoulder.

"How does that fit?"

Michael talked, but with the mask on, it could only come out as mumble. Edgar shook his head, and instead Michael just gave him a thumbs up.

"Excellent." Edgar exclaimed, looked back at the manager who was leaning against a rack of Star Wars games, looking a bit dazed and somewhat hopeful that this would bring some new business into the store. As past owner of a few retail businesses, he was aware of one thing when it came to marketing; crazy works.

The two of them proceeded out the front door, walked across the parking lot and stood out by the curb in full view of the street. Immediately cars began to slow down and through the slits in his for eyes in his costume, Michael could see some of the young kids in their seats pointing, yelling and bouncing at the sight of them.

It wasn't long before it had its needed effect. As more and more cars slowed down, Edgar barked out orders to increase the presentation. At first he pretended to chase

Michael, then they reversed roles. Then they pretended to climb out onto a tree limb, balancing carefully along the curb.

Through his costume, Michael could see the attendants at the wing bar in the shop next to the game store, laughing and pointing. But as the cars began to slowly pull into the lot, they suddenly realized their own windfall. The workers watched the lot fill up quickly, and ran back to their stations, put on their plastic gloves, adjust their hats and inspected the springs on their tongs. The owner of the wing bar, in his own ingenuity, hand wrote a discount promotion on the back of his "NOW HIRING" sign, and taped it to the front door.

He smiled as cars continued to pull in, the parents trying to control happy and pointing children and then glancing at his promotional "1/2 price on wings with Game shop purchase." sign.

Soon, the gesticulations were beginning to heat up the suit, and Michael felt the sweat beginning to rise on his back, run down his spine and pool at his waistline where the elastic of the bunny pants kept a tight grip on his hips. Giving Edgar a time out hand sign, Edgar was also slightly winded, and they both stopped to catch their breath. Michael bent over slightly if only for his t-shirt to absorb the running river of sweat down his back. When he arose, he looked straight at an old German man with a stern look and an envelope in his hands.

Apparently the old man had come out of the bar a few stores down, and Josef was now confronting Michael, his missing granddaughters husband, while the world looked elsewhere. Josef stared at him hard. Michael was certain he couldn't be recognized with the mask on, but the intensity of the stare made his heart skip. In a defensive reaction, all he could do was wave his paw side to side.

Jacob glared hard at the character in front of him. Despite the cloak of his disguise, Michael clenched his teeth and felt his spine go rigid. He remembered that look of iron which bored away all pretense of courage and confidence.

It wa a look familiar to him. First seeing it as a younger man just dating Andrea, he was able to charm the parents over an Easter celebration, yet he noticed the old man quietly sitting at a corner table, seemingly oblivious of the large number of family members pooling in corners of the rooms, or out on the deck enjoying the first true sunny day of the year.

Almost with a scowl, Josef glowered over the crowd, settling at times on him. The old man occasionally sipping the glass of brandy in front of him he was playing with. Grabbing a beer, Michael strode over to the corner where Josef was seated, intending on sitting across from him, yet losing his nerve to sit as the stare grew more intense.

"I'm Michael Planck." He offered.

"I know who you are." He replied back without a smile. "You're the boy dating my granddaughter."

"Yes sir. She's great."

Jacob nodded. "Do you have a job?"

"Ahh... yes. I sell carpeting part time, and when I'm not doing that, I work for a friend selling cars."

"So a job here and there."

"I guess." Michael said beginning to get defensive. "It brings in some money."

Jacob slowly shook his head then stood up and the stare came into play. "Get a real job." Then he stood up and walked away.

"Get a real job." The old man ventured with a harsh deep tone that Michael had heard too many times. The words hurt him now as much as it hurt him then, and he lost his momentum displaying his character, and had to be nudged back to work by Edgar.

In response, Michael bowed slightly motioning with his arms that Josef was free to pass. Michael wanted to say something, give him a message to take back to his wife and kids that he was okay, but he knew the intensity of the people looking for him, and any knowledge they had of his location may hurt them, not to mention what the gang is doing to find him.

He watched as Josef strode past him, unknowing, glancing at his watch while walking towards the train station some blocks away. Michael watched him for as long as he could, until he felt the tap of Edgar's furry paw on his shoulder, encouraging him to begin the show again. As the children gleefully entered the store, the glass door now propped open to handle the volume, his own kids crowded his thoughts. The pang of guilt began to get physical as he felt a pressure on his chest as the longing to see his kids grew stronger.

When the time had expired, they shuffled over to the front of the store and dismantled their costumes. The removal of the rabbit mask caused him to take in a huge rush of fresh air. Having gotten accustomed to the staleness of the mask, he was almost dizzy with the sudden rush of clean oxygen. The sweat that pooled on his back, chilled as he exposed his open shirt to the elements and in a pile, they left the costumes by the front door, where the girl had already backed up her car and opened the trunk to return them to the rental store.

Before they were in the store, the owner came out counting twenties. Smiling, and a bit relieved, he gave each of them $100, thanking them profusely, he said he had no problem if they would come back some other time and do this again.

Edgar scoffed. "We'll talk." Was all he said as he rolled the bills over his thumb, slipped them into his pocket and walked back into the parking lot. Before they had left the site, the owner of the wing shop ran out with two huge buckets of wings and some drinks. Nodding their thanks, they left the lot with their spoils.

"Come with me." Edgar said, and they turned the corner and walked off of the strip and into the long blocks of residences that lined the streets. They walked about 4 blocks, then in the middle of the 5th, Edgar reached in his pocket for his money, took out a napkin that he had and wrapped the money in it. The house they were in front of to had a small front yard, and a narrow grey sidewalk which lead up to a narrow front porch.

With certainty, he walked onto the porch and flipped up the lid of the long black metal mailbox by the door and reached in to pull out a blue pen. Scrawling something on the outside, he placed the pen and the money in the mailbox and closed the lid.

Walking back out to Michael, he shoved his hands in his pockets and stood there with his head down.

"Paying a debt?" Michael asked.

"Compensating."

Michael looked around and with his insight, tendered a guess. "Which house is yours?"

Edgar looked up and pointed to a kelly-green house with clapboard sides. It was very similar to the one they were at; same style, different color, built at the same time, by the same builder.

Michael took the initiative, and walked over to the front of the house. He could see the drawn shades, hiding the darkened interior.

"When was the last time you were in there?"

"I left after the funeral. Never went back in."

"Why not?"

"She's everywhere in there. Pictures, clothes, half finished puzzles, cut up magazines. Can't go back in yet."

Michael could see the fear in his face, and smiled back at him.

"I'm hungry." Michael said, as he slowly walked up the sidewalk and towards the front door. He waited for a shout from Edgar, but when it didn't come, he continued to the front steps of the porch. Hesitating, he then took the first step – the stiff boards popping and snapping under his feet, then a second step, and then the last one.

Looking ahead, he could see a hanging swing lazily moving to and fro from the wind. Deciding to play it cautiously, he walked over to the swing and sat down on one end, the chain snapping tight, the wood groaning, unaccustomed to the weight.

Bringing his tub of wings onto his lap, he placed his drink next to him and proceeded to eat selectively choosing the wings he wanted out of the bucket.

Edgar stood on the sidewalk and watched Michael get comfortable on the porch swing. After a few moments he to walked to the front stairs and walked onto the porch. Hesitantly he proceeded to walk towards the swing. Michael was oblivious to his presence, not acknowledging him as Edgar sat down next to him, and set up his own meal.

"My dad made this swing." He said before he began to eat his own lunch.

Michael nodded, throwing a bone into his tub, and reaching for his drink. "What else did he make?"

"Lots of stuff. It's all in the house."

"Can I see it sometime?"

Edgar seemed to think hard for an easy answer. "Sure," he answered. "Some day."

Michael grinned at him and held out his drink. Edgar took the cue and raised his own, tapping Michael's in a congratulatory salute.

Smiling, they ate quietly, swinging slowly, and enjoying the afternoon.

Julia stared at Hayden.

Hayden stared back at Julia.

Julia adopted an indifferent, somewhat annoying

look, while Hayden sat quietly across from here with an expressionless face.

"You said that we can leave anytime we want?" she began.

Hayden nodded.

"I think I might do that. I don't think I'm getting anything out of this anymore."

Hayden shrugged softly.

"I'll probably just go back to that lousy situation with my mom and whoever she's hanging around with now. Of course as soon as I show up he'll probably have his hands all over me."

She paused.

"She'll tell him about how I see colors with music, and how crazy that is. That usually sets them off. Makes me fair game."

She scowled and laced her fingers in front of her, shifting from a sitting position to one where she was on her knees, hands straddling them.

"It's not fear." She said softly. "I'm not in trouble, I haven't done anything wrong." She followed in a pleading voice. Glancing at Hayden, who returned her stare, she saw his eyes soften. The quiet between them became less awkward now, more familiar. "I just don't want to go back there again. To another shitty situation where I have to be on guard all of the time. I just want to be…." She hesitated looking for the word. "Safe."

Silence.

"I suppose that I could see my older sister in Sacramento. She was always good to me when I was a little girl. She's like 5 years older than me. She was from my mom's first boyfriend after my dad left. My dad is in Florida now, I think. Anyway, she used to bring me little presents and stuff, you know, dollar store stuff. Nothing important, just the crap the little kids play with."

She chuckled a little.

"I remember now telling her that I saw colors when I saw music and instead of calling me crazy, she used to bring a guitar to my room and strum. Then she would ask me what colors I saw. When she did that I stopped being afraid. My mom never believed me, but she did."

Julia was quiet now. Thoughts of the past tumbled through her mind, she smiled weakly at the pleasant ones as her eyes grew red at the sad ones.

"I don't want to go alone." She said. "I'm not afraid." She said defensively, then quickly added. "It would be good to be with someone, so I'm not by myself."

She unlaced her fingers and made two fists. 'DON'T' and 'DO IT' were pushed together. Looking at them side by side, she tapped the knuckles together and then looked at Hayden who smiled back politely.

"You understand?" she asked.

He nodded his head slowly and then reached out to her fists and surrounded them with his own. He held them tightly. "Did you hear yourself and understand?"

"Yes." She said softly.

He released her hands, and then reached into a small leather bag next to him, while Julia slipped a necklace of beds out from under his shirt. He opened the bag and held it out to her. She gazed down into the pouch, thought for a second, then reached in and pulled out a yellow one.

The gang leader sat at his usual table, only this time not alone. Across from him sat an individual who had something to give.

"So I understand that you have something for me." He asked very skeptically as he laced his fingers and set them on the empty table in front of him. Like a gate, it sent the message that this must be worthwhile, otherwise it remains closed.

"There is someone you are looking for. I know where he is."

"Really." The leader started, glaring calmly into the man's face, assessing value and intent.

"What makes you think I would want to know something like that. Why would I need to know where someone is. I have access to all kinds of information. My guess is, is that you want something from me." He leaned forward. "Where you ask what I'm willing to give, I am going to ask what you are willing to lose."

But the intimidation didn't seem to work, the man sat there unflinching calmly staring ahead with his arms across his chest, protecting his own assets.

"You're looking for Michael Planck. He owes you a lot of money. I know where he's at.

The boss shrugged his shoulders and smiled slightly. "And for this information you would want what in return?"

"One day I am going to ask you for a favor."

The boss slammed his hand on the table and leaned as far forward as he could. "This isn't a fucking movie asshole! Don't fuck with me!'

Caught off guard, the man flinched and fumbled for the words, any words.

"Ok…ok." He blurted out, his eyes widening, and he inhaled sharply.

"I want a plane ticket. That's all, just a plane ticket out of here."

"To where?"

"Florida, Tampa to be exact. One way?"

"Why?"

"I have family there. I need a fresh start. Things are better now, I'm better now and I want to get out of here."

He paused.

"Look, you win twice, you get your guy and I'm out of your hair." he offered.

He thought for a second. A long second. He turned in his seat, away from the table and stood up over the man, breathing heavily.

"You go when I tell you, right?"

"Will it be in the next few days?"

The boss looked over to his associate, then back at the men; and nodded. He took a pen out of his jacket. The associate presented the man with a pad of paper. Setting it in front of him, he leaned in very close.

The boss was quiet, calculating. "I tell you what. You bring him back here in 3 days, to this bar, to this booth." The boss stood up and pulled his dress shirt tight. "and there will be an envelope waiting for you."

Without hesitation, Daniel nodded quickly in agreement.

"Well done Daniel. I'm sure we'll be hearing from you soon."

The structure of the restaurant was still there, a blackened hull with the windows cleaned of broken glass. Those stores that weren't severely damaged by the earlier explosion had recovered and reopened. The bulldozer that had been there earlier had scooped out the parking lot debris and the junk from inside the restaurant and emptied it into about a half dozen truck size dumpsters, which had then been hauled away.

The door was parked far out into the empty lot by the semi's, waiting for new brick and steel support to come in so it could finish the outer demolition and allow the new frame to be assembled.

The parking lot was half full on this Sat. morning. Two police cars were parked end to end and in front of them was a cardboard table with a large map of the forest preserve taped to it. It had been subdivided and marked with colors and numbers. On the corner of the table was a stack of smaller, easier to carry maps the officers placing a pair of handcuffs on it so they wouldn't blow away on the sporadic gusts of wind that invariably showed up.

The day itself was cool, but sunny. A perfect day for a hike in the woods to look for birds or a missing person. About a hundred volunteers had arrived and they mulled around swapping stories about earlier searches they were on and drinking coffee from thermoses. Peter had arrived early to be sure everything had been set up correctly. He watched impatiently as the crowd slowly gathered, looking at his watch frequently, wishing 9:00 would get here soon.

Finally, when it was close, he gave the order to begin, and the police officers began to get the people organized into groups to assign them into search teams to look into specific areas.

"Detective?"

Peter turned and saw the ranger in full gear standing behind him. He already had a map in his hand, and was smiling with eagerness.

"Great to see you here." He said in greeting. "How's your back?"

"Just fine, he replied "I did a treatment right before I came so I could last the day. Listen, I will take a group myself into the area here to search. It is a little overgrown and some people might get lost.

"Ok." Peter replied and gazed at the area circled on the Ranger's map. "That's the Truman Glen area."

"Right. I have actually gathered some people together that have hiked this area frequently to search in that spot. We should be able to cover it pretty quickly."

Peter gazed beyond the ranger at the loose gathering of people. He thought they seemed odd, looking like they had been camping outdoors for some time. The bald man with the tattoos on his wrist seemed intelligent, but some of the others; like the girl with the ski hat and the letters on her fingers seemed a little off. No matter he thought, they all have eyes, as he turned to the rest of the group and tried to install some sense of order.

CHAPTER VII

Josef reached up to the top shelf of his bookcase. Feeling with his hands for the wide binders, which he could see from the ground but were hidden up close, he finally found the one he wanted. Using his strong fingers, he was able to pull it out a little at a time, each time releasing to get a better grip. Finally, when it was out far enough, he was able to grasp it firmly and pull it away from the stack.

Smiling from his victory, he held the wide book out in front of him as if he had found the true Bible itself. The thick leather cover had a warm odor which stirred the images and his mind raced as the memories began to reappear.

This particular volume had what he needed. The other photo albums had pictures that told the stories of Cynthia's childhood, the vacations they all took and the accomplishments they all had as his family grew together and shared their lives.

The photo album he held now was different. It held the clues he needed from the past. His past. He slowly opened the cover, creaking with resistance at having to be disturbed after being alone for so long. Once opened the yellowing plastic sheets lay still, holding their specific pictures in tight 5" x 7" pockets.

He didn't have much, only the first ten pages or so of the fifty available were full, but they told some of the story. Some were document photos he was able to obtain from some government agencies that had the information. There in front of him sat his mother and father, holding stilled expressions in being documented for the bureaucracy. Other photos of his family he was able to get from distant relatives, friends, and neighbors that he was able to reconnect to, whose pictures had somehow survived the war. On one sheet there were two photos badly creased, the white backing bleeding through the print, of himself at eight years old, and his older brother Otto at school. They were photographed at the gymnasium for some event. Both of them staring blankly into the camera. The picture had been salvaged, and he was able to retrieve it from a widow who found it in her husband's keepsake box. Josef went to school with her husband when he was a boy, yet never remembered him until the letter came with the pictures. The widow was pleased she had found him. There were many others she was looking for that had disappeared forever. Luckily the photographer had written their names on the back to verify it.

Also in the books were photos of the factory his father owned, the house where he grew up, and a photo of the piano teacher smiling pleasantly and eating an orange on her front steps. He was pleased she was smiling in this one. The bombing caused her to lose her mind, and in reaching out to friends who know her, they told him she never smiled or spoke again. She died soon after the war.

Suddenly, he turned the last page and the thick, blank pages lay stretched before him like a clear canvas, plastic sleeves crackling with newness as he flipped through them. Holding the book tightly, he rose and left the bedroom where the book had been stored and headed towards the kitchen.

At the dining room table, he set it down gingerly and went to the stove where the water was starting to boil. With a cup of hot tea, he returned to the beginning of the album once more, leafing through it twice more before stopping again at the vast emptiness at the end.

He looked up and gazed out his dining room window. Children were out playing in the no-man's-land between the houses. He watched them quietly as they laughed and ran around each other, falling over in sheer delight. Reaching into his pocket, he pulled out the spoon and set it on the pictures. A bookend, he thought. But was it the beginning, or the end.

Reaching down to a chair next to him, he presented the file folder with the current photographs of the city that he had taken in the library. He had purchased larger storage, full-page sheets for these, and he slid each one carefully into them doing his best not to tear or fold the corners. After complete?? the half dozen or so pictures, he then opened the binder rings and placed the new pictures at the bench. With a snap, he closed the rings and just for effect, he gazed at the pictures again from the beginning, ending as desired at the last picture he had placed.

Michael sat quietly on a log near the path and watched the body swing back and forth turning slightly in the gentle wind. He and Edgar had run across it as they were heading along the path toward the bus stop. The man was wearing a bright yellow dress shirt and dress pants with a sharp crease, easy to see from the path.

While Edgar went back to the compound to notify someone, Michael chose to stay. He noticed the phone, keys and wallet stacked neatly on a nearby stump, but he didn't need to look at the identification to know who it was. He had kown him casually through his daughter's kindergarten class. Someone who always seemed together and prepared, organized; yet Michael remembered talking with him in the corner of the room in numerous class events and he came across as overwhelmed and very anxious about his job and wife and the 4 kids he had. "Stressed out" he heard and "going through the motions" was the other one he remembered.

But as he watched the stilled man, his arms straight and toes pointed, his face grey and blue in death, he wondered what would have caused him to make this choice. This wasn't an accident that just happened. Michael could see the plastic torn and crumpled on the ground from where he took the packaging off a new white cotton rope. Where he had slung the rope over a healthy limb, tying it off onto a tree trunk not far away, just under the crotch of a low branch so it wouldn't slip. He could see the branches piled up just high enough that when kicked away he hung just above the ground, far enough that the distance was unreachable if he changed his mind. The stray arm of the branch he was attached to, groaned from the weight of the corpse, seemingly in despair from the burden hanging from its lowest branch.

As he waited, his mind drifted back to the man's family. His wife and kids were certainly concerned about him. There was no use cutting him down, the dead man had been there for a few days, so for at least a couple of days the man's wife and kids were wondering where he was. Perhaps going to the store for something and never coming back. Perhaps scoping out an area to do this. This area is some distance from the parking lot, and they just searched this area a few days ago looking for him. Surely they could have found him. Maybe he was with the search party, using that as a pretense to plan this. Looking for the right spot, the right time, the right tree.

Sitting awkwardly, he shifted on the hard surface of the log, and stared at the ground. If he left a note, maybe that would be easier for him. In tossing around the damage he had done to his own family, he could only pacify himself with the fact that this way was worse. At least his family knew, mine doesn't he thought. At his family knew, mine doesn't, he thought.

The sound of rapid footsteps rustling the leaves of the path broke his concentration and Dr. Coda showed up with Edgar.

With a look of deep concern, he stared at the hanging man, then took out his cell phone and began a brief text. "Do we cut him down?" Edgar typed.

The doctor just shook his head. "That's someone else's job. I'm notifying the ranger now." After sending the alert on his phone, the doctor noticed Michael on the log being very quiet. "This happens occasionally," he said. "Some people just get overwhelmed and this is the choice they make." He sat down next to Michael. "Death is inevitable. I don't understand why people willingly choose to expedite it." He began.

Michael turned to face the doctor. "Has suicide ever crossed your mind?" The doctor replied, "You mean because of my cancer? Yes. I think about it from time to time. But I balance it with a sense of purpose. The skills that I have I can use here."

"Why here? I mean, why did you come here?" The doctor looked thoughtful. "Because not long ago I was looking for a tree. I had just been diagnosed, and felt the unfairness of it all. I had dedicated my life to helping people. I can't count the times that I had to put family and friends off to help total strangers. For what? To have everything taken away. Didn't seem fair, and the only way that I thought that maybe I could win was to try to have the last word. Leave when I am ready, on my own terms. But then I began to realize that it was selfish to take away the gifts that I have, the lives I can still save while I can still help people. One day I was visiting a patient in a retirement home when I had an attack of acute pain. I had left my pain pills in my jacket pocket at my office, so I was sitting in this patient's room, and she could see that I was suffering. She went to her bedroom and came back with a bag of herbs. She brewed a pinch of them in water in the microwave, which took only a moment. Within thirty minutes of drinking the brew, the pain was literally gone. In fact, I was pain free for the remainder of the day. I asked her for the source of the herbs, and after meeting the messenger, he brought me back to this camp where I am needed much more than in the outside world."

"What about Hayden? Where did he come from?"

Dr. Corda smiled. "That's his story. You need to ask him about that."

"So the pain is totally gone?"

"No, it comes back in the morning until I drink the herbs. But then I am pretty much pain free for the rest of the day."

"So is the cancer gone?" "No, it will take my life, but I have a plan, and I am not ready yet. Not until I'm sure that I have given everything I could."

Having completed his story, the doctor stood up, offering his hand down to Michael to assist in pulling him up to his feet. The tattoos of bands on his wrist were inches away from Michael's hand. "What's with the bands? he asked.

"All part of the plan. Now let's get out of here. The ranger is coming with the police and we can't be here."

Peter tossed his phone on the desk and dropped the stack of papers under his arm in the trash can next to it. With a loud crash, they landed there in a heap; torn and folded scraps, a food sack, and sheets containing lists of unread instructions of what to do with evidence that was found.

Plopping down in his chair, he leaned back, rubbed his forehead, and exhaled heavily. Hearing the commotion, a rookie walked over to his office his arms crossed across his chest, stopping at the door; shy, but inquisitive.

"So. Not so good?" he commented.

Peter just shook his head. "It was like herding cats."

"That's bad."

"I tried to break them into organized groups, but the people who thought themselves "professional searchers" couldn't agree with the methods of the other members, so I had to constantly keep switching them between the groups."

"Then I had to show them what a police line was, and that you had to do it slowly and far apart. That worked for about 10 minutes, and then the groups started to gravitate into cliques so they could talk about past searches, and then those groups that were going too slow or too fast…. and they were yelled at by everyone else.

"So no luck."

"Nothing. Not a shoe, a shoelace or a fingerprint. I know it's a cold trail, but I thought for sure I would get some sort of clue; but nothing."

He held up his finger to make a final point. "I will tell you this, though: Of all the trouble I had, that ranger kept his group in line and efficient. I spent no time with his group, and he ran it flawlessly. They were in and out of the 'Truman's Glen search area in no time at all."

"Any luck with them?"

"No, they struck out also."

"Well, you tried," he said as if a condolence. "I guess in hindsight, it was a long shot." "What's left to do now?"

"Nothing at this point, unless some new evidence

181

shows up that points me in a new direction." He exhaled slowly and closed his eyes. At almost the same time, his cell phone rang. Reaching into his pocket, he checked the caller ID. Holding the phone close to his ear, he quietly listened.

"He did." He replied.

The rookie having no idea who he was talking to, or what the question was that he was responding to, waited patiently.

Michael continued, "No, I'm fine. Just a tough day.….. Just, just frustrating….no, I haven't forgotten.…..right, two o'clock.….. and you have a ride to the airport? Good. OK, see you then."

"Planning a trip?" the technician asked.

"No, just my dad. He's flying back to the 'homeland'." "Where's that?" "Germany. At the end of the war, he came over to the states. Now he has this need to go back."

"Permanently?"

"Well, he's over 80, so I'm guessing so."

"Is he going by himself?"

"No, he is going to stay with his sister, my Aunt. They have it all worked out, I'm just staying out of it. Waiting for the information to trickle to me."

"You going to miss him?" Peter shrugged.

"Hardly saw him while I was growing up. Hard to miss someone you never really knew."

"Did he travel a lot?" Peter thought carefully. "He was into 'opportunities and acquisitions.' Don't know much beyond that."

"Well, some dads are like that." the rookie offered.

"Yes, there are." Peter replied, then swiveled the chair toward the desk, signaling to the rookie that the conversation was over.

"Well, if there is anything that I can do, just let me know," the rookie replied hopefully.

"How old are you?" Peter asked.

"Twenty-two," was the sharp reply, answering as though this was not the first time that he was asked that question. "Your dad still around?"

"Sometimes." the rookie replied.

"So I get it." he then turned and walked back into the squad room.

Now that he was alone in the office, he tried to conceptualize everything. The case was now in purgatory – that is easy to manage. Put it on a shelf, dad was now front and center. At times like this, he truly missed his mom he thought. She understood him, managed the approaches and knew what to say and when to back off. Now with just the two of them one on one, with no referee it was difficult. His younger brother was of no use, those two were already connected through the business and they had their own wavelength. Business only. He was the one who had to be there now. Thinking long term, he realized this may be the last time. From here on out it was just occasional phone calls and a card for his birthday. He squinted as if in pain, and opened his desk drawer to gaze at Sara's picture. "You would know what to do," he said.

With some sense of pride, Michael stood at the edge of a foundation bed, and viewed the work that he had accomplished. In neat squares perfectly bordered by concrete, the plants were trimmed back, beds weeded, and ground turned in some areas to allow for seeding. Ahead of him were only a few more lots to prepare, the seeds and leaves striking the correct presentation for harvest.

He smiled, adjusted his shoulder satchel and walked over to the next lot to begin work. He was only there for a few moments when he heard the rough sound of footsteps on dry grass. Looking up, he saw Julia walking toward him, a broad grin spread on her face. She wore a t-shirt with the sleeves cut off, showing off the broad, developed shoulders of an athlete, yet she somehow moved with an aura of feminine vulnerability.

"Mr. Wong told me to come over and help you finish." Michael shrugged his shoulders, and began his work in one corner of the foundation. "Do you want me to start here?" she asked, motioning to an area not far from his starting point. "That's fine," he said offhandedly, and with that cue, they both began to work with the plants.

As the day wore on, he would straighten up to relieve his back, and at that time glance over everything around him, including Julia. She seemed oblivious to his presence, but when the roles were reversed, he noticed her looking at him through the corner of his eye.

They continued at a steady pace, each keeping up with the other, sometimes drifting close, and then a few yards apart. By the time lunch rolled around, she had worked herself close by. They took their break with the others, meeting up at the eating area. As sandwiches and water bottle were handed out, Julia reached the front of the line first, and handed duplicates of everything to Michael. They headed to their usual circle, only now Julia sat a little closer to him than she ever had before. Despite being a little uncomfortable with the familiarity, he said nothing and didn't move away. But in his head, an alarm was starting to ping, and he wasn't sure what to make of the situation.

"Heard any good music lately?" Daniel asked as he sat down. Julia grimaced and just ignored the question. As the group talked without any participation from Julia, she was naturally excluded and proceeded to finish eating in silence. Witnessing the dynamics between Julia and Daniel, Michael assumed that there was a jealousy thing going on and decided to ignore the entire situation, despite the alarm still ringing in his head. A few minutes later she leaned in even closer to him, whispering in his ear that she still had ½ of her sandwich left if he wanted it. She looked at him from a few inches away, with open eyes and a welcome smile. He smiled back and declined the sandwich, wondering where Daniel went off to and willing away the now constantly ringing alarm bells.

Swallowing the last bite of her meal, she wiped her hands on her jeans, and placed her hand on his shoulder, using it to help her to push herself up to stand. Her hand lingered on his shoulder, and her fingers dug into his shoulder deeply. "Ready to go, partner?" she asked. Nodding in approval, he too stood up and grabbed his water bottle, throwing their trash away and putting a few feet between them. As they started walking back to the plot, she seemed to suddenly lose her balance and fall into him. He instinctively grabbed her arm to steady her, yet that didn't prevent her from bumping into him. The warmth of her arm, caught him by surprise with how pleasant it felt. He realized he hadn't been close to anyone in weeks and it was a welcoming feeling. It was his turn to linger and as he left his hand on her arm to steady her, he felt her other hand on top of his. She glanced at him, he looked quickly and turned away, releasing his grip, yet feeling her hand grasp for his. Subtly, her palm slipped into his. He didn't push her hand away, and in another moment, her grip tightened.

In his own quiet way, he removed his hand and returned to work, her work space much closer than before. He realized, then that he didn't mind her closeness.

Josef sat in the chair for some time. Rolling the decision around for weeks, he was disappointed in himself for not being brave enough to finalize it. He had gathered all of the information, shared it with his friends, watched with envy as Randolph was the first to pioneer the road back. Still, he couldn't seem to pull away. He wouldn't make the final leap. Thinking about Andrea and the grandkids was difficult, but they would survive, the family was tighter now, even without him.

Hearing the doorbell ring, followed shortly by a quick knock, he went to open the door and saw a trio consisting of 2 women and a man. All of them wore shorts and oversized tee shirts with the man wearing hiking boots and a Australian bush hat. One of the women held a clipboard, while the other stood ramrod straight behind her. "Hi. We're sorry to bother you, but are you Mr. Josef Zimmerman?" began the lady with the clipboard. She spoke politely, almost in a singsong, yet he knew this was some sort of business by the way she looked directly at him, like a bass stalking a minnow. Behind her, the man opened his stance and crossed his pipe cleaner arms seemingly ready in case Josef bolted away from the door to avoid the confrontation.

"Yes." He replied.

"I'm so sorry to bother you, but we are the Landscape Committee for the Brookdale Subdivision and we are following up on a slight violation that may have been committed."

Not sure what to say Josef stared at each individually, then shrugged.

She continued, "It seems that you have planted a tree in your backyard. Is this correct?"

"Yes."

They collectively seemed to sigh, now that there was admitted guilt.

"Okay, well um…. You see, you can't do that."

"Why not. It's my yard, I can plant anything I want."

"Well, no, not really." At which point the man and the enforcer looked at each other and rolled their eyes at the ignorance.

"You see you have to request for a tree to be installed."

"With who?'

"With us."

"Okay, I want to put in a tree in my backyard."

She chuckled slightly and looked away. "It's doesn't

work that way. You see you need to fill out this request form." Which was the first page on her clipboard, which she detached and handed to Josef. Once we have that, we can proceed with the authorization."

"Ok, wait here and I will fill this out and give it back to you."

"Actually, we needed that before you planted the tree. Which brings up another problem, the three looked at each other and rolled their eyes again. "You put in the wrong tree."

"It's the tree I wanted. How can it be the wrong tree?"

Snapping another sheet from her clipboard, she presented him with a list of species, their size and cost.

Glancing at it, he saw his tree on the list and pointed to it.

"Here it is… a red maple."

"Yes, I see, but it is too small. The community requires a 3" caliper tree minimum."

Josef stared at her a little perplexed.

"Caliper is the width of the trunk." And as if on cue, the man pulled out a ruler, held it perfectly horizontal in front of him, and pointed to the 3" mark with his free hand as if educating on a children's program. "Yours is less than 1".

"Then I will plant two more."

"I'm sorry, you can't do that, you can plant only one tree, at this size." And as if to close the deal, she pointed with her pinky finger to a line of numbers. "and this is how much it will cost."

"Four hundred dollars!!"

"Yes, that is correct, but you get a one-year warranty."

"If you water it." The ruler man added in an oddly high-pitched voice.

"That's ridiculous."

"Well," she began with a shrug. "These are the rules we all live by to stay in this community."

"So you are saying I can plant a tree if it is ok with you, that has to be a certain type you approve of, and it will cost whatever you say it will?"

The enforcer crossed her arms, ready to jump in at any sign of trouble, the ruler man had a firm grip on the lower end of the ruler; paper cutting edge facing out. Josef looked at the three of them and replied. "I've seen this before."

"Please review everything and let us know what to do." They slowly began to fade away from the front door. When they were a few feet further away, she threw her last grenade.

"Oh, and you have a month to get rid of the tree. If you don't the landscaper will remove it and we will charge you $75.

Once they reached the front sidewalk, Josef could see them congratulating each other on a successful intervention. While Josef slowly closed his door and walked back into his living room.

He placed the forms on the coffee table in front of him, plopped down in his favorite chair, then reached for the cell phone on the end table next to it.

Dialing a memorized phone number, he waited as the

phone to purr in predictable bursts. On the third ring, a woman's voice welcomed him.

Leaning back, he stared at the ceiling as he began. "Hello, Lufthansa?"

It was a long day, but complete. Working together they were able to clear out the day's plots and also get a head start on the next day's work. With rain forecasted the next day, it maybe a washout, and Mr. Wong didn't want to get behind.

With a sense of pride, Michael walked to the end of the street and threw his bag down with the other, Mr. Wong clapping words of encouragement as all of the workers filed past doing the same. For a moment Michael time to reflect. Placing his hands on his hips like conquering general, he looked over the fields he had worked, now satisfied with his accomplishment. He also marveled at his own condition, lean from the exercise, his body chelated from the diet he had at home, and his skin brown from the sun. In the past, he was exhausted at this point in the day, now he just felt refreshed.

Julia was right next to him, less enthused by the day's work, more interested in getting back to camp and cleaning up. "I hate pulling those thistles." She said. "They cling to my socks and are a bitch to get out." She stamped her feet in frustration at having pulled out as many as she could, yet still feeling the sting.

Michael smiled and nodded, "Comes with the territory I guess."

With all the work completed, the troop of workers

began to walk back up the hill to the camp. Behind them, on the horizon the clouds were beginning to form, and a cool breeze spurred by the moisture, blew through them.

"It's going to rain tonight for sure." Julia said.

"It seems so." Michael answered. "Definitely sleeping late tomorrow." And she smiled. In the past, they had walked single file on the trail, now she was next to him. He felt her bump into him in the narrow stretches, and brush past him while he held up the low branches.

Reaching the edge of the camp, they split up, her with a wink and him with a smile as they went to finish the remainder of their work duties at the camp before it got too dark. His was stacking the wood supply for each of the campfires. Covering each cord with the tarp to prevent them from getting wet as a mist began to form, he was able to get back to his tent before the rain began to fall at a steady rate.

He was just settling in, when he heard a rustle at the front, and the flap covering the entrance flew open and closed quickly. She was there in front of him in a huddle on the floor, wearing an oversized sweatshirt and thin spandex. Her hair was wet, but he knew it was because she had just washed it, the warm smell of soap filling the hut. She pulled her knees up., holding then tight with her hands, the lettering on her fingers especially bright after being cleaned. Her sweatshirt had shifted slightly exposing her shoulder, the tattoo of a nautical compass exposed, with a clearly defined large 'N' strongly standing out, and a bold arrow pointing up. He could tell it was the one emblem on an evolving canvas.

"I forgot," she said meekly, "my hut leaks in the rain." She shrugged at the fact. "Can I stay here tonight?"

"Fine with me." He replied, and gave a ready smile that he hadn't expected.

"It's supposed to be cold also, we can be together, stay warmer?"

"I'd like that." He replied.

She half stumbled, half crawled towards the middle of the hut, where there was a large collection of pillows, to lay down on. He located a few folded blankets in the corner, and spread them out. His hands fumbling with nervousness and his breath short. His heart was racing with anticipation, yet in his brain there was a thin fog of doubt, and it began to seep into his consciousness, no matter how hard it was to push it away.

Once everything was arranged to how she liked it, she laid down on her side, her back to him and her knees pulled up. She pushed back her hair over her shoulder exposing her ear and neck. Taking the cue, he shuffled over and spooned behind her, feeling her body slide into his. With a sweeping wave of his arm, he covered them both with the blanket. He placed his left arm over her head, while with his right, he hugged her tightly. She nuzzled against his arm, while her hips began a slow grind against him.

At first, he felt a response to her, but then it began to fade. Feelings of guilt began to rise out of the fog of doubt, like rocks on a shore. He laid there very still while she continued to get aroused just by his presence. Then, unintentionally, he saw it, glistening like an obelisk. His wedding ring suddenly seemed to be shining brightly like a beacon, and he stared at it hard.

It felt heavy now, and he pushed his thumb against it, feeling the warmth radiating through it. Rubbing his thumb against it, he began to push on it; hard. So hard that he began to feel the bone of his finger. Slowly he closed his fingers over the thumb holding it tightly in a fist.

Sensing his distraction, she slowed her movements to a stop, glaring at the fist in front of her face. Suddenly fearful that it could come crashing into her eye. "Look….." he began. "I like this, I like you. But I can't let this go where I think it is going."

"Ok." She said faintly.

"You can stay here, but I think it is better that I slept over here."

He began to slip away, then blurted out as a final excuse. "I have a wife and kids."

"But you left them." She replied.

"Not really. I miss them and I am realizing I want to go back. So it's not you. It's me"

She lay there awhile, and as he settled down at the edge of the hut, he watched her back as her breathing slowed and he was sure she was asleep. Closing his eyes, smiling at his decision, he slowly slipped into a deep sleep.

CHAPTER VIII

M ichael woke up alone. Because of the sunlight slicing through, he knew it was morning. He could also hear the rest of the complex rousing for the day. The thud of fresh wood being set on latent coals to bring the fires back to life. The laughter of people as they gathered together in work groups for the day. The bark of a dog that someone found, yet cannot keep because of the rules against animals, even though it has already been here a week. All of the sounds of an active village, one with a heartbeat and a soul of its own.

Tossing aside the blanket, he changed into fresh clothes from the small collection he had, and slipped into the open air. The morning chill he felt on his cheek revived him and the sharp cool air pushed out the staleness of the hut with one deep breath. When he first arrived, the early start took some getting used to, now it sparked his adrenaline, and fueled him for the morning awakening. Having changed, he pushed aside the tar and entered the complex.

Slowly he walked towards the nearest fire where someone had brewed coffee, it's strong aroma making him more vibrant as he got closer. When it's power was in reach, he was approached abruptly by Dr. Coda, waving his hand to get his attention, as if trying to hail a cab.

"Michael." He yelled, then coughed with a deep rasp from the stress; then proceeded to walk towards him. But there was something odd about him today. Something wasn't right, his gait seemed off, and instead of a steady gaze, he seemed to look down at the ground before standing and addressing him.

"Yes, Dr." Michael answered.

"I need you and Daniel and Edgar to go into the city to do some deliveries and pickups.

"Sure." Michael said, then paused at noticing a redness in the man's eyes, and a grayish tint to his skin.

"Are you okay?" he asked.

"I'm fine." The Dr. said, then brushed away the question with a wave of his hand, like shooing away a fly. "Just off this morning, I will be better later after I've had some medicine. Please get to Edgar and let him know when you will be ready. He gets nervous when he doesn't have his day scheduled."

"Sure thing. Oh, by the way," Michael asked sheepishly, "have you seen Julia?"

"I know she was with Hayden this morning and then she left."

"Where is she working today?"

Dr. coda seemed perplexed by the repeat of a question he thought he had answered. "She left. She gathered the things she needed and left the village."

"She's gone?"

"Leaving the village and not planning to return would definitely count as gone, or as I put it twice before; she left."

Tired of the redundancy, Dr. Coda then turned and walked after another group of people concerning himself with their needs and ending his time with Michael.

Michael seemed dazed at the news, not quite sure how to process it, then looked at the ring on his left hand, the finger was swollen and bruised from the night before. Sweating again as he did the day it was slipped on his finger, promising never to take it off.

After breakfast, Edgar was easy to find as was Daniel. Both were just finishing up with the supplies, when Michael strode up.

"Perfect timing asshole." Daniel sparked up. "We get everything together, then he shows up.

"Shut up Daniel." Edgar said as he split up the bags amongst the three of them. "You weren't exactly a lot of help either."

Michael smiled at his defender, appreciative of the remark.

"Now today we need to split up. When we get to the city, Daniel you and Michael go to other Old Town stop, I will hit a few of the Riverdale places and we will meet back at the usual time.

Michael and Daniel nodded in agreement, then silently the three of them marched out of the compound following Michael's lead. Within minutes they were swallowed up by the foliage and heading off to their destinations.

As planned, they got off the bus, then split up after a another few blocks, Edgar headed in a direction Michael was familiar with, while Daniel seemed to follow a familiar path, but then seemed to go into a new direction that Michael didn't know. Edgar wanted to go back separately, so they both knew to to wait for him.

"Are you sure you know where you are going?" Michael asked.

Daniel just nodded, then seemed to quicken his pace, more intent on getting to the first stop. Obliging, Michael stepped up also, yet in his head there was a brewing anxiety. Something was off. He wasn't sure what it was, but he felt it. Not sure how to address it, he just continued as directed; but something in his head was telling him not to trust Daniel.

They made it to the first stop – a hospice, where the exchange was made as usual, and Michael began to relax a little, perhaps this whole Julia thing had knocked him off his mark as he just shrugged off his feelings as paranoia.

On the way to the second stop, Daniel proceeded down the block, then turned sharply at an alley. He walked down knowingly, yet Michael was beginning to get a stronger feeling. One that was telling him, not only not to trust Daniel, but to get out of the alley. Still he shrugged it off, following along quietly until they came to a grey steel door in in the center of a brick wall that, due to the smell of stale beer and the stickiness of the ground, was at the back of a bar.

"I don't recognize this place." Michael commented.

"We don't stop here often." Daniel said, then knocked,

rather pounded twice, on the back door. Waiting a few moments, the door then swung open, and large thick man in a butcher's apron and heavy black moustache, glared at the two of them. Then Daniel nodded and motioned for Michael to follow him. Hesitating, they strode past the man, the two of them walking into a dark hallway, the door slamming hard behind them.

Edgar stood in front of the house and slowly studied every feature. He scanned every shudder, the posts on the porch railings. Mrs. Flanagan must have gotten her money because the lawn had been mowed as he instructed. They even trimmed the bushes on the side of the house. Nicely done he thought.

Standing in front of the house from the sidewalk, he stared at the small house and studied it and how he felt. Slowly, deliberately, he began to walk up the sidewalk, to the porch stairs where he continued up the incline without hesitation. When he was on the porch, his hand instinctively reached into his pocket and took out a small ring with a plastic yellow tab with a single key.

Raising it to the lock of the front door he slid it in, and turned it until the bolt slid away. Releasing the key, he then grabbed the knob of the door, turned it as slowly, hesitated; then pushed the door open.

It swung open easily, without the groans and drama of a haunted house, but of an obedient servant waiting for a task. He stood there and inhaled the air of the home. It was dusky and the rooms were dark from the enclosed shades, but he could still smell the candles his mother would set out, and in some odd way, feel the warmth from the kitchen.

Gauging his own feelings, he stepped forward and into the home, the floorboards creaking with submission to their sudden use. The living room was the front room, it's worn upholstered sofa and chairs gathering dust in silence. Above the fireplace he saw the lace doilies on the mantle, which framed a setting of 'glass bird' figurines along its length. Brilliant reds of cardinals and blues of jay's stood out sharply despite the speckling dust trying to darken their plumage. On the small tables in the living room and on the top of the piano, were the pictures. Photos of his mom and dad, both old and young dotted the scene, with twice as many pictures of him at seemingly every day of his life surrounding them.

With confidence now, he strode through the living room towards the dining room. As he walked passed the table and china cabinet, he placed his fingers on the surface and dragged them across the varnish, leaving thin trails in the dust, like a farmer plowing his field.

The shades were drawn tightly, the darkness deepened by the nearness of the houses on either side. It was darkening in the center of the house. What little light was coming from the kitchen in the back, and he headed towards it. This was the last room on the first floor and he stood in the center, gazing at the closed cabinets and the stilled appliances that were softly waiting for a command.

The windowshade facing the backyard was half open and he had a close view of the short cut grass with the dandelions slowly invading the turf from the edges. 'At least he could have pulled a few weeds.' Edgar thought to himself. But then he shrugged realizing that he could be the one doing it instead of the neighbor.

A narrow sidewalk ran along the fence just to the side of the yard, and it led to the aged single car garage in the back of the lot. It blocked the alley, and it's sun bleached white paint was beginning to crack and peal, a sure sign that age was beginning to exact a toll.

Looking around the kitchen itself, he smiled at the square wooden table in the center filled up the small kitchen so completely, there was barely enough room to pull out one of the four wooden chairs situated around it. From a design point, nothing fir. It was all early hodge podge. Some of it even coming from the alley on the advice of neighbors. But to him it reminded him of quiet dinners at home in the warmest room of the house. He distinctly remembered hearing the mixer from his room and running downstairs, knowing that his mom was making cookies. Showing up mid task, he would push himself against the steel edge of the counter, trying to get a glimpse of what she was making. The counter was yellowish with red and white speckles, and the spilled flower made it look like stars through the clouds.

Having just learned to spell he would take his finger and write his name into it, his mother placing her warm buttery hand on the back of his neck while giving him a doughy spoon with the other.

"When will it be ready?" he would always ask.

"Soon." she would always say.

Exiting the kitchen he returned to the dining room,

and gazed into the china cabinet. Spying something in particular, he popped open the center door and reached in with both hands to grasp a porcelain hen and the small yellow chick placed next to her. The mother hen was leaning down, it's wings slightly open with it's head cocked to one side, as if listening to the chick. The small yellow bird on the other hand was looking up, it's mouth open in full chirp.

The hen had one flaw, which was why it was in the china cabinet to begin with. One of the tail feathers had been snapped off by a small boy some 20 years ago and never found who just wanted to play with them.

Reaching in, he grabbed one figurine in each hand, then pushed away one of the side chairs of the dining room table with his foot, and slid into it. Holding them gently, he slipped his thumbs along the smooth cool glass finish, put his head down and softly cried.

The narrow hallway was dark and Michael's eyes had a hard time adjusting. His other senses seemed to be spurred by the loss of sight, and he could hear Daniel's thin boyish voice far away in the background. Suddenly, the weight of the bags he was carrying faded away quickly as they were taken from him, and a firm hand on his arm seemed to lead him further down the darkened hallway.

Blinking hard to gain his sight back, he began to see shapes and the outline of the hallway as he was led towards what seemed a dead end. Almost reaching the end, he was then steered away, and they burst into the light of a large dining room with multiple tables and a long bar. At the far end, a large picture window revealed the street in front of the bar, with it revealing the atmosphere around it with its own natural light.

As if suddenly thrown into a conversation, Michael noticed the bartender out of the corner of his eye. Turning to look, the bartender then gazed back, sat down the case of vodka he was stacking and quietly ventured towards the back room where he wouldn't see what was about to happen. A shadow by the window suddenly glared into view. He saw Daniel standing by a long table where a middle aged man sat very quietly, not looking at either of them.

"Sorry." Daniel said as he stuffed an envelope into the front of his pants, pushing his shirt down in front of hide it. "But this is my shot at a second chance." He stood there awkwardly, holding his arms uncomfortably by his side, his fingertips rubbing together nervously. "Couldn't pass it up." And with making point, he took two strides towards the front door and was gone.

There was now only himself and the man in front of him. The henchmen beside the man was now gone. Fading away like a monster before the light, leaving only the two of them in the large dark restaurant.

"Have a seat Mr. Planck." The man said, his voice echoing into the darkness.

Not seeing any alternative, he released a heavy sigh, almost out of relief, Michael walked quietly over to the table and slid into the booth. He turned and looked outside, longing to be on the street, and not here where his unknown fate was being decided.

"We meet at last." The man said, with a half grin. "You have been very elusive." He then smiled, as the bartender reappeared with two clean glasses and a fresh bottle of brandy. Placing one in front of each of them, he then turned away and returned to the room behind the bar.

Reaching for the bottle, the man twisted the cap and poured each of them to shots worth of whisky.

"I don't drink." Michael lied.

The man shrugged. "Let's just say it is for medicinal purposes. I'd drink now, so there is less pain later." The smile was gone now. This was a dictum, not a suggestion.

"You were very difficult to find. Amazing how you vanished so completely. Every time, I've found my debtors, but you, you were tough. If it hadn't been for your friend there, I may not have found you for maybe what…. a year?"

Michael shrugged. The fear was gone from him now. Like an inmate waiting for his sentence, he sat there quietly. No defense, his arms by his side.

The man let the silence gel between them. It made every motion and every noise a thousand times louder. Michael looked up and saw him glaring with satisfaction, almost pride.

"Despite all I have been through, all the effort I have exercised, I will respect the brilliant move you made and give you an option I have never given anyone before."

He then produced a set of garden hand pruners, still wrapped in their plastic. With a deft move, he pulled it from its plastic and then set them down on the table in front of them.

"I am going to allow you the choice of which two fingers you would like me to remove."

Michael felt a heaviness in his chest and his fingers go suddenly numb. He stared at the tool in front of him, the oil on the blade clear with its newness.

Slowly the man pushed the drink towards him, the glass on the surface of the wood table, grinding softly. "Like I said, this will take the edge off the pain."

Michael tried to be brave, but his knees began to shake. Looking at him directly, he could see the cool confidence the boss had, and it terrified him even more. "So I chose what to lose and that's it?"

The boss smiled. "That's where we start."

Michael reached for the glass, realizing his hands were trembling also when the edge of the glass struck his teeth.

"Look, the boss began. ""You seem like a nice guy, and I know you've made a bad mistake,….an egregious lapse of risk speculation let's say." He leaned forward, lacing his fingers together and placing his palms flat on the table. "But you owe me, and you don't have it, and you ran away." He leaned forward slightly, tilting his head towards the table. "Those are bad things and you need to be the example for all of the others. No one can get away with doing this to us, otherwise," and he leaned back into a slouch, opening his arms as if exposing the whole world. "we lose respect, and that's worse."

"So is this going to kill me?" Michael said in defiance, a question with a hard edge.

The boss seriously thought for a second, then answered quizzically. "Probably not." Then smiled.

Michael took another sip of the liquor and tried to somehow think of a way out of this mess, but in the back of his mind, he knew it was over.

As Michael took a long swallow and felt it burn its way down his throat, the boss reached into his pocket and pulled out is phone. Highlighting the screen, he went directly to a list of names and punched the asterisk at the first one.

Waiting patiently, he gave Michael a weak smile.

Connecting, he began to talk in a low voice. "We found him." Michael heard him whisper as he reached out for his glass. Suddenly he halted; his brow furrowed and he bent his head down low to his chest.

"But we need to set an example, otherwise this will continue and we will be pinched." He listened intently. "But you had to leave, they were finally onto you….." He reached for the drink again, this time grasping it fiercely. "Alright I'll do it. But only this one time." He pushed hard on the screen and stared at it solemnly. Taking a hard swallow, he slipped it back onto his pocket, and then glared and Michael. "Today is your lucky day. You're being set loose, no strings attached. Just the promise never to come here again."

Not waiting for a second invitation, Michael slid out of the booth, suddenly reaching back for the remaining shot of whisky, gulping it, and turning to leave.

"Wait!" the boss yelled with an eruption. He too slid out of the booth and slowly approached Michael who had his hand on the front door handle; his heart racing, the noise from the street outside calling to him to escape."

"Who do you know?" the man asked intently.

"Guess I have a guardian angel." Michael uttered, then slipped out the front door and disappeared into the crowd.

The park in Cologne was full of small children playing joyfully in the late afternoon sunshine. They frolicked around the swings ad climbing cubes oblivious to the well-dressed old man on the bench. Parents initially were wary, but deciding he was harmless went about their business keeping an eye on their children and sharing the news with the neighbors.

Rudolph stared at the phone, thinking about the call he had just made to his son, and wondering about Michael's future. He couldn't tell Josef what he had just done; it was impossible. It would have pulled too many loose strings, unravelled many stories and exposed harmful truths. But it didn't matter. No one would ever know about his second chance he had just given a young man. No one except his son Ernst, but he would never tell. He was family.

Rudolph smiled to himself, lit a cigarette and crossed his legs casually like a man who had all the time in the world. Besides, everyone deserves a second chance, let's see what he does with this one.

Michael ran and ran until he thought his lungs would explode from gasping for air. He ran down a few blocks, then turned a corner where there was a crowd of people. He immersed himself in them, then slid into an alley and behind a dumpster gulping for breath and sliding down the brick wall, stretching his legs out as far as he could to stop the cramping.

As he struggled for air, trying to calm his pounding heart, he turned his head up to the sky, closing his eyes as he felt the warmth of the sun on his face. Slowly his system began to slow down, and his breathing returned to normal, the anxiety began to subside and he began to realize he was free. He could go home now. He was never closer to death than a few moments ago, and yet he walked away. Scared, but untouched and forgiven, He had a second chance, and now he could go home, no strings attached. He didn't have any animosity, towards, Daniel. The boy was only trying to survive. He got his second chance too.

Confident that he wasn't being chased, he rose awkwardly, stamped his feet and slowly walked out of the alley. Lowering his head, he blended in with the crowd and began the long journey back to the camp.

Reaching the camp alone, he mingled through the occupants, only now he looked at with a fresh perspective. His time was up, and he could sense it as the longing for his kids became obsessive and he ached for the touch of his wife. He went to his hut; and scanning around it realized there was nothing here that he wanted. But he took a long look anyway at the last place he would ever call solely his own.

Satisfied that he had all he would need, he then closed the flap and walked away. Heading towards Hayden's tent, he took in all the sights and sound around him. They seemed fresh to him now that he knew it was time to leave.

Approaching the hut, he pushed open the flap and walked to the center where the thick pile of rugs awaited. Seated comfortably in the middle, Hayden took one look at Michael, then held his hands out, open palm facing up "Welcome Michael."

Michael sat down as he usually did, Hayden smiling at him all the while.

"It's time for me to go."

"I know." Hayden replied, and he reached into a hidden pocket just inside his tunic. Carefully, he pulled out a necklace, Michael's necklace. He held it, dangling between the two of them, allowing Michael to see the color transition from sadness to contentment with each added bead.

"It's been an interesting journey." Hayden replied.

Michael shrugged. "I feel better. Things seem a little clearer now."

"That's the intent."

Michael held his hand out, Hayden dropped it into the open palm.

"Isn't this where you tell me to go in peace?"

Hayden scowled, "I've told you before this isn't a movie. What do you think I should say?"

Michael thought for a second. "Don't fuck it up again."

Hayden chuckled. "Let's go with that."

Michael switched the necklace to his other hand, then once again held out his right hand. "Thanks again."

Hayden grasped it, and shook it firmly. "My pleasure."

Late that evening Michael walked through the village, nodding to a few acquaintances, unbeknownst to them, for the last time. He searched for Edgar briefly, but hearing that he had returned very upset, he instead left a note in his hut thanking him for all his friendship and support.

With what little he had, he embarked through the woods with only the light of the full moon. Having traveled it many times now, he easily avoided the trails pitfalls, taking a slightly different route to get back to the restaurant where it had all started.

After a few hours, he emerged from the brush at the edge of the parking lot where he had disappeared with Edgar's help. The semi trailers were still there; the restaurant was not. A perfectly square pad of concrete in a sea of asphalt was all that remained. Pipes protruded, isolated and cut off, in clusters like branches. Some dumpsters remained, overflowing with specific materials, one with steel, another with concrete. A building returned to the basic materials used to create it.

The lighting in the parking lot was solemn and dim, and with the distant traffic noise, it seemed a little surreal. People were still putting small teddy bears, ribbons and flowers laying them on the concrete like a sacrificial altar. He smiled to himself at the sincerity, and walked quietly passed them as he strode towards the sidewalk.

He still looked the part of a vagrant, although did not have the requisite shopping cart full of bags, or an overstuffed suitcase full of forgettable relics. As such he walked the few miles undisturbed, with the exception of the one squad car that approached him slowly, then sped away.

As the neighborhood became more familiar, he felt his step get stronger, and at the approach to the monument sign leading into the subdivision, he felt a familiarity as if he never left. Being late at night, everyone had settled down inside for the evening. Warm glows from windows shown out some of the light, and with little outside interference, it was all he needed to navigate his way through the soft curves in the road.

Reaching the third intersection, he recognized the names, and decided to turn down the lane to walk passed Josef's townhouse. From the angle of the street, he was able to glimpse behind the house, and when he got closer to Josef's, he had to stop and study what he was seeing.

In the backyard, just off of the deck, he saw the little tree Josef had planted growing straighter then he had remembered, with a canopy of thick leaves, and new growth pushing out from all the branches. He wasn't surprised at the trees vitality, Josef was attentive to all the things he cared about. But what amazed him was the ½" thick, linked chain wrapped around the trunk and then secured off with a tight padlock. The 8' chain linked fence with barbed wire on the top surrounding it was an additional deterrent in case anyone was able to get the tree freed from the chain.

In its tiny enclosure the tree seemed remarkably secure. Only the Liberty Bell would have more protection. It distracted him slightly, only to be caught off guard by the sight of two thick suitcases packed by the front door. He walked closer, approaching the empty driveway, stopping half way up and sliding his hands into his front pockets.

As he processed what this meant, Josef came out slowly, dressed neatly in pressed trousers with a new shirt and dull tie. He too approached slowly, also processing this specter that had magically appeared at his door.

"Michael?" he said softly.

"Hi Josef."

"My God you're alive." he then outstretched his arms and swallowed him. "I never thought I'd see you again." He released and stepped back, staring at the changes I him.

"Your thinner, and I barely recognized you under the beard, but it really is you."

"It's me alright. No doubts about that.'

"Where have you been all this time."

Michael thought for a second, then dismissed the question with a wave of his hand. "I'll tell you someday. It's really kind of boring."

"Well, it will have to be long distance. I am heading out of the country for a while." He shifted awkwardly. "Going back home to Germany."

Michael nodded in agreement." I don't blame you."

"Ya. This place is changing a lot. The world here

is different now. I know it will be different there also, but its......."

"It's home." Michael said, finishing this sentence.

"Yes." He agreed. "I mean with the tree and the house and the old neighborhood fading away.... You know." Josef said pressing home a sudden point. "even the work is different. It used to be you worked in a factory or an office building. Now .... I saw two guys a few weeks ago dressed up like cartoons. What kind of a job is that?" he pleaded.

Michael shrugged his shoulders his face contorting to a false sense of disdain. "I know, what kind of a person would do that for a living. So demeaning. How long are you staying in Germany?' he began quickly changing the subject. It was Josef's turn for indifference. "I don't know. I'm staying with an old friend. I will stay as long as they will have me."

"Forever?" Michael joked.

Josef thought for a second. "At my age every day could be forever. That's why I need to do this now."

"I've been thinking a lot also." Michael said. "I've made some bad choices. Took a lot of people for granted. I need to fix that."

Jopef smiled."You should stop talking to me and go home. Your family misses you."

"We will miss you to."

"I'm not so important anymore."

Silence. Josef held out his hand. Michael grabbed it. Josef frowned slightly in surprise.

"Firm grip and callouses." He smiled. "Seems like you have learned something."

After the handshake, Michael turned and walked down the driveway. Turning the corner at the intersection, he began to get anxious at the thought of seeing his family again, not noticing the taxi to get Josef to the airport passing him on the way to the house.

Faster than he realized, he was there, at the intersection, suddenly fearful he would lose his nerve, he bowed his head and continued forward, until he stood in front of his home, familiarity now seemed to embrace him. With what seemed another day in his old life, he walked through the house from the neighbor's lot. Reaching the back yard, the same preschool madness prevailed. Same toys, same disarray. Stepping around the playhouse, over the Hot Wheels tricycle and around the sandbox, he approached the large potted plant positioned by the patio door. Leaning it forward, he reached under it and found the key. Still there after all this time.

Pushing it deeply into his palm, he approached the back door to the garage and slipped the key in. In a moment he was in. Despite the darkness, he found his path to the interior door. Used a second key under the paint can on a shelf nearby he slipped into the house.

The kitchen was lit by the light over the oven. It always was. While standing quietly by the door, the smells and the warmth of the home began to loosen him. As he had hoped it was late enough that everyone was asleep. Having slipped into the house unnoticed, he made a mental note. 'Got to get a dog."

From his vantage point, he could see into the adjoining family room along with the chaos in the kitchen. He wasn't used to this, then he reminded himself it had been a single parent household for some time. Things are different now.

Confident that he hadn't awakened anyone, he made his way towards the basement stairs, being cautious not to step on anything to cause him to break his leg. Luckily deep in the basement that he had his own bathroom, and a separate closet to handle the overflow of clothes from the bedrooms. Equally lucky, when he glanced at the closet next to the bathroom, he realized she hadn't thrown away his clothes yet.

Walking into the large tiled bathroom, he closed the door quietly, and turned on the light. For the first time in months, he was able to get a full look at himself. His clothes were ill fitting and worn as all-hand-me downs were, slowly his eyes gazed at his new self, with his skin darkened by the sun, and his eyes pronounced by the thickness of his beard and the shaggy mop of hair overflowing over his forehead and ears. No wonder Josef was taken aback. He didn't recognize who he was either.

Stripping down, he threw his clothes into the corner. Sliding into the shower, he turned on the water, rejoicing in its heat on demand, and marveling at the smell of soap. His soap. Scrubbing himself raw, he could see the darkness of the water at his feet as the forest began to runoff and flow away. He washed his hair twice, just for the enjoyment of it, the steam rising and cleansing him as he regaled in it's rejuvenating qualities.

Once clean, he bowed his head under the shower head, letting the water flow down his back. He could feel it seeping into his bones reviving him. At first he closed his eyes, but then opened them to look at the necklace of beads hanging off his neck. They reminded him. The would always remind him.

Feeling a brief sensation of cold water, he realized the hot water heater was almost empty, and turned off the water. Opening the door to the shower, he grabbed a thick towel from the shelf and wrapped himself in it. After drying he wrapped it around his waist, then standing before the fogged mirror over the sink. He swiped his hand a few times over its surface to clear away the condensation. Calculating his next move, he reached down and picked up the small garbage can at his feet. Setting it in the sink, he then opened the top drawer on the right and took out a small pair of scissors.

With a deep breath, he then began to cut away at the beard that had swallowed his face. After sometime, he was able to trim away at the growth getting its density down to a thick layer of stubble.

Moving the can back to the floor, he then turned on the hot water tap and let it run for a few minutes to heat up. Luckily the hot water recharged quickly, and once it was warm enough, he lathered up and began the process of reclaiming himself. From the same drawer as he retrieved the scissors, he pulled out a slaving can and razor. Just for good measure he also brought out extra blades.

The shaving took longer than the shower, but in the end, he saw himself again, yet still different. Staring at the mirror, the sink under him strewn with hair and small tuffs of shaving cream he could see the corner of his eyes were now deeply creased, by the sun his chin and nose more pronounced and leaner from the change in his diet. Also new and improved, he thought to himself. With a weak smile, he slipped out of the towel and softly opened the door to leave the bathroom.

Reaching into the closet, he pulled out a ten year old souvenir t-shirt from Cancun and lacking any underwear, a pair of swim trunks from the same early period in their lives. Fully clad and comfortable, he ventured up the same stairs with as much caution as before, and then turned the corner to go up the stairs to the bedrooms.

His son's room was the first one on the right. The door was only half closed, and he slowly pushed it the rest of the way to see the small sleeping boy bundling tightly in a comforter, only his thick blond hair nested squarely in the center of the pillow. An orange dinosaur night light let up the room, so he was able to move around the plastic noise making booby traps on the floor.

Reaching the side of the bed, he stared down at the sleeping child, smiling to himself at how amazing the boy was. Bending over, he kissed him on the forehead. Moving by instinct the sleeping child rolled over on his back, eyes closed, arms outstretched. Taking the boy's hand in his own, he held them tightly against his cheeks, as if trying to latch onto the child's soul with just his touch. The coolness of the boy's hands made him press them tighter against his cheek, in his mind he wondered how he could have ever left this child and promised him never to leave again.

The boy stirred once more, pulling his hands away this time. Without protest, Michael let the hands slip away, then kissed him on the forehead. One last time as he drew the blanket back up to the boy's chin, tucking him in tightly for the night.

Slipping away, he quietly entered his daughter's room next door, it's walls illuminated by a pink princess night light, and as before pushed her hands tightly against his cheeks, kissing her softly on the forehead.

At the end of the hall was the master bedroom. The walls seemed much longer than it really was, and when he got to the door, he looked around at the place he missed the most. Looking over the disarray, his eyes quickly settled on the shape buried deep in the sheets. Quietly approaching the bed, he pulled away the sheets softly, and slid beneath them. She was on her side facing away from him, yet turned her head around, gazed at him with half opened eyes, as she felt the weight of the bed shift. "It's just me." he said quietly. She responded by placing two fingers over his mouth and turning towards him. "I missed you Mike. We'll talk in the morning." He felt her nose push into his neck, she inhaled deeply as if absorbing his scent and all of his aura. Her arms reached around his chest, her fingers latching deeply into his ribs. He responded by placing his hand on her head, burrowing his nose in her hair, and falling into a deep sleep.

CHAPTER IX

<u>Edgar</u>

Watching the children play at recess, Edgar crossed his arms and watched their interactions keenly. The thirty or so boys gathered on the asphalt of the school playground were almost indiscernible in their matching uniforms, the only distinction was the hair, and with most of them being blond, he had to look intensely to make sure he was seeing the O'Brian kid and not the Kelly kid.

The fenced-in playground helped keep their wanderings in check, but someone had to be responsible to make sure no one wandered in, and today was his turn. Everything seemed to be normal, the usual kids were hanging together, playing the typical games, no abuse, terror, just the usual Alpha male territorial bullshit by a bunch of 10-year-old boys.

However, as he gazed over his flock, he saw something unusual today. One of the boys that seemed to always be smiling and joking seemed to be distant, and at times he pulled away from the others and stared out past the fence as if trying to see something no one else could see.

Walking slowly over to the boy, he placed his hand softly on his shoulder. Startled the child turned to see Edgar looking down on him, his eyes wide. "What's wrong Aidan?" You seem to be distracted today?" Edgar asked softly.

At first he said nothing, then looked down.

"It's just my dad. He's really sick and I'm scared he's going to die."

"Is that what they told you?"

He shook his head no. "But my grandma got really sick and went to the hospital just like him and she died."

"But wasn't your grandma really old?"

The boy nodded again.

"There are things that happen to us that we cannot control. That test us, and make us realize what's important but we have to understand that we cannot change what's meant to be. Have you talked to your mother? How about your older brother, have you talked to them?"

"I'm afraid to. I'm afraid it will make them sadder." I'm trying to be strong so they won't worry about me."

"It's one thing to be strong, it is another to let people know how you feel. I think if you talk to them you'll realize that they're scared and sad also. When you're all honest with each other, there is strength in that. You have a strong family and they live very close. You can count on them."

The boy leaned his head on his shoulder, his soft hair resting on the back of Edgar's hand.

"Remember, we are all family here and we are here to be there for you."

The boy sniffed and placed his hand on Edgar's wrist. "I know," he said softly. "Thank you Brother Edgar."

Julia

Julia sat quietly in the cab of the truck, the purr of the Freightliner adding background noise to an otherwise silent night. The seat was worn and uncomfortable. A second rate cab owned by a third rate self-employed hauler. One the side of the semi, there were tape scars from the constant taping over of the new owners, whichever one employed him that given week.

"Wants some?" the man asked in a low voice. With his large blackened fingers grasping the Dixie cup, he held it out for her. She could smell the whisky which helped cover up how he really smelled; like a wet sweater lying in a filthy drawer.

She shook her head no.

"Whatever." He replied, taking the shot himself, then pouring a little more in from a 5th bottle between his legs. Setting the cup on the dashboard, he then screwed the cup back on the bottle, and slipped it between the seat next to them.

"Where you coming from?"

She shrugged. "Nowhere."

"You just want to get to California. Right?"

"Yes."

"Looking for a new start right?"

"Yes." She agreed, then looked out the side window at all the other trucks lined up at the truck stop for the night. A few other women were coming from the diner, going from truck to truck knocking on the doors, some getting an open invitation after being checked out by the drivers, many others ignored, passing on to the next one.

"Well, here's how it works," the man, about in his fifties with thin grey hair and spaced out yellow teeth, shifted stiffly in the driver's seat as he reached around his girth to pull a thick wad of bills from his front pocket.

As he moved, the stuffy smell like a well-worn sock began to seep throughout the cabin. Whereas it didn't sicken her, it made her very aware of who and what she was dealing with.

"I'll take you there, but I need something in trade. You see, I need to relax for driving that far."

He slipped a twenty off the top of the roll he had and placed it on the dashboard in clear view of the two of them.

"To get me to relax, I'm willing to pay a little extra. Girls' got to eat, right?"

"Right." She said softly.

"So here is the offer. You take that and I will tell you what I want you to do to help me relax."

Julia looked at the crumpled moon sitting on the dashboard. It's torn and blackened shape a perfect fit for the interior ripped and chipped from years of neglect.

"So what will it be?" he asked.

His eyes stared hard at her. He was hungry now and intended to cash in on a deal he now felt was inevitable.

She looked out the window again, at the diner this time with the waitresses serving hot plates of food and patrons cutting up slices of meat and warm bread. Tall glasses of soda and free water with huge slices of pie to finish off the meal. As if on cue, her stomach growled and she tensed up in trying to control it. She looked at the money again, hesitant.

The man reached into the roll, placing another twenty next to it. "Is that better?" he said.

"Please turn up the radio." she requested and the sound of country music filled the cab and a blue haze began to surround them, blurring out the darkened dashboard and torn fabric seats. She placed her hands on her lap, gazing at the lettering detailed over her fingers.

'Don't' slipped under her leg so she wouldn't see it. 'Do it' snatched the money and closed the deal.

Dr. Coda

Dr. Coda was helped to his cot by Mr. Wong and another young man. He then added more incense to the burner, sending the aroma in a flush into the tight air of the hut. Mr. Wong was on one side as they laid him down on the thick layer of pillows. He reached for the quilt by his side, but with a quick grasp of the wrist, the Dr. prevented him.

Even in the dim light of the hut, Wong could see the ashen color of the man's face, his eyes sunk deep into their sockets, a cool perspiration on his brow.

"I'll get Hayden." Mr. Wong added.

"No need." Dr. Coda answered and tried a weak smile. "You can do this."

"Do what?" Mr. Wong said in the quivered voice of a scared man.

Dr. Coda reached it his chest and unzipped the thick sweatshirt he had put on that day. In the light, Mr. Wong could easily see the bulge beside the breastbone, extended now 2-3 inches above the rib cage.

"This is the beast within." The Dr. Added. "This will kill it." He added pulling on a thick rawhide rope looped around his neck and disappearing somewhere on his side. Pulling on it, a small leather satchel appeared

"Give me your hand."

Hesitant, Mr. Wong held out his hand but was scared to place it anywhere near the bulge.

"Don't be frightened, It's only a tumor. A cancer. It has been my tormentor for a year or so and I am now ready to be free of it.

Opening the satchel, he dropped three pills into Mr. Wong's hand. A black one, and red one, and a green one. He then closed the fingers around them, making a fist.

He then pulled the sleeve up and exposed his tattoos. "This is the code. Green one first – thar is the painkiller. Wait two minutes." He pointed to the number in the band. "Then give me the red one. That is the tranquilizer. Wait five minutes." Pointing to the net number on the band.

"Then I give you the black one?"

He nodded. "I will be unconscious. So you must open my mouth and break it over my tongue. Just add a dropper of water. And that's all you need to do."

"Is it a poison?'

"I prefer to call it the gatekeeper."

"I don't think I can do this. We should get you to a hospital."

His eyes grew soft and he gave Mr. Wong a knowing smile. "They can't help me now. They never could help me. Follow the code. You're not doing anything that I wouldn't do myself."

As Dr. Coda's breathing grew more even. Mr. Wong found himself getting dizzy from the short breaths he was now taking.

"Relax, just follow the code. Please."

Mr. Wong steadied himself and took the green pill from the trio. Dr. Coda opened his mouth, slipped hit on his tongue and took a quick sip from a glass nearby.

Quickly the pain killer took effect, and Mr. Wong watched his time. When two minutes were up, he administered the second pill in the same fashion. A few second alter, Dr. Coda closed his eyes and his breathing became very shallow.

Mr. Wong looked at the final pill in is hand, ten at the band on Dr. Coda's wrist his nonverbal command to give the final dose. He doubted. Sudden fears of his own soul began to seep into his consciousness. His father's voice seemed to appear behind his ear whispering his moral code. Ad for the first time he listened. He knew he now had to complete this, not because of his own conscious but because he was going to complete a cycle, helping to end a life which was ready to be ended. Following the instructions on the main's wrist, Mr. Wong waited the five minutes, then pushed the man's chin down to open the man's mouth. His breathing was till shallow, and his skin had a warmth to it despite the ashen appearance.

When he had opened it as far as he could, then held the capsule over it. He thought he would feel al final hesitation, but it didn't emerge, and he snapped the pill just above the man's mouth.

The crystals fell quickly and he could see them glisten on the man's tongue, but then quickly fade. He reached for the eater, but there wasn't any need for it. There was enough moisture to activate it and suddenly Dr. Coda's breathing became irregular. He opened his eyes, they were glassy, yet fixed on something far in the distance. Another quick dry gulp followed, and he exhaled, Mr. Wong swore he heard the mane Vivian. He watched and waited for another breath which never came.

Hayden

With the bell ringing, there was the sudden explosion of doors flying open, the hustle and chatter of students and the slam of an occasional dropped book. Immediately checking their phones, they shuffled blindly through the hallways and out the doors as they transferred blindly from class to class. For those lucky enough to have classes on the same floor, it was an easy transition. Between floors it was a little more hurried, and between buildings it was clearly frantic to get from one seat to another in the ten minutes required.

In the Psychology Building, there was a calm, almost sedate atmosphere, as if pumped into the air were the sedatives recommended by the accomplished physicians within. In a northwest corner of the second floor, the doctors of the Human Behavior were beginning their afternoon lecture of the day. Dr. Piedmont finished the computer set up of his power point presentation oblivious to the students trailing in behind him. As if by instinct, he completed his set, closed his laptop at the table at the front of the class and opened a black three ring binder next to it. Flipping through the tabs, he settled on the section he was going to lecture on, the then turned to face the class exactly as the bell rang.

"Today we are going to study an area that I have been researching for some time. In fact, I'm currently in charge of a study group that has been progressing very well supplying a great deal of data on a paper I expect to complete soon."

He then shifted slightly and glanced at his notebook once more.

"It is called the power of silence and how people can reflect upon their own behaviors if allowed to listen to themselves. It is one thing to ask someone to tell you how to deal with our problems, it is another to be silent as the listener, and let them process what they themselves just said. Sometimes the answer is something they know all along, but could not accept.

A student in the back raised her hand, speaking as the arm went up.

"Dr. Piedmont, how do you measure your own progress in each case if you aren't measuring what they are saying?"

"Good question, ok, and please call me Hayden. I use something simple and easy to relate to.....beads.

Peter

Peter stood by the side of the large lake, gazing at the sailboats as they skirted across the surface, their sails adding vivid yellows, oranges, and blues to a dull green surface.

With his hands in his pickets he seemed reflective, but in his head he was analyzing the details of a new missing person case. Deep in thought, he didn't the shorter, stocker man dressed in black walk up behind him.

When the stranger stood next to him, Peter then acknowledged he was there.

"Hi Ernie."

"Peter." The man said softly.

"Glad you could make it."

Ernie smiled, "Things are a little slow at the office."

"Heard through my sources that you found my boy and let him get away." He turned to look at Ernie, shoulders square, hands still in his pockets.

"Don't know what you're talking about." Ernie said glanced at Peter, then shrugged. His way of saying yes.

"Let me guess. Dad had something to say about it."

"Old man is getting soft in his advanced age. Maybe going back to Germany changed him.

"Perhaps."

"Either way, thanks for letting him go home."

"In some ways it was best. A body sends a strong

message, but draws unneeded attention that not even you can cover up."

It was Peter's turn to shrug.

"Either way, got a new one maybe you can help me with."

"Okay." Ernie said slowly hesitant on the request as he tapped out a cigarette from a box he pulled out of his shirt.

"Looking for a young man, missing about 3 months now. Blonde hair, medium build, edgy, first name is Daniel. Any idea?"

Ernie placed a cigarette in his mouth, reached for a lighter in his pocket and snapped out a flame. Pulling a deep breath, he lit it exhale as he replied. "Not a fuckin' clue."

Printed in the United States
By Bookmasters